Praise for *Guillotine*:

"Fast, fun, and frightening, *Glass Onion* meets *Saw* in this savagely on-point thriller." T. Kingfisher

"Reading Delilah S. Dawson's *Guillotine* is like watching poetry smash a bottle against someone's face. Fast, stylish, very bloody, and unapologetically brutal, this is a straight razor of a novel that slices to the core of class resentment with power and grace. This novel will leave a slug trail of blood in your brain, and you'll be happy it did." Gabino Iglesias

"Deliciously brutal and stiletto sharp. *Guillotine* is the eat-the-rich horror you've been waiting for." Rory Power

"Gruesome and laced with a delightful sense of humor, Delilah S. Dawson's *Guillotine* showcases the author's brilliant nerve and clever wit. A compelling and intelligently written shocker." Eric LaRocca

"*Guillotine* is at once a vicious reckoning of wealth and power, and a feminist fever dream led by a protagonist you can't help but salivate over. I would follow Dez Lane straight into Hell." Katrina Monroe

"Murderously cathartic — or perhaps cathartically murderous? — *Guillotine* continues to prove that Delilah S. Dawson is a must-read must when it comes to sinister, twisted tales. Elegantly constructed, ticks along with thrilling tension, won't you come take a trip to the island? (Also serves as an interesting companion piece to *Bloom*, but you didn't hear it from me.)" Chuck Wendig

"Sometimes the line dividing the Haves from the Have-Nots is as thin as a razorblade or blunt as a sledgehammer, but in Delilah S. Dawson's cruelly capable hands, rest assured, it's gonna hurt no matter what. Her taut novella testifies revenge is a dish best served flambéed, or sous vide, or pounded into an absolute pulp. In *Guillotine*, you gleefully get all three... and then some." Clay McLeod Chapman

"A pitch-dark, sharp-toothed romp with a rich vein of gallows humour, *Guillotine* is a gory, uncomfortable treat for anyone who's ever wanted to eat the rich. Blending the glittering world of *The Menu* with the disturbing underclass of *Us*, Delilah S. Dawson's latest novel is another triumph." Ally Wilkes

"*Guillotine* is a tight thrill ride of horror you can't put down." V. Castro

Also by Delilah S. Dawson

It Will Only Hurt for a Moment
Bloom
The Violence

THE BLUD SERIES
Wicked as They Come
Wicked as She Wants
Wicked After Midnight
Wicked Ever After

THE HIT SERIES
Hit
Strike

Servants of the Storm
Midnight at the Houdini

Mine
Camp Scare

Star Wars: Phasma
Star Wars Galaxy's Edge: Black Spire
Star Wars Inquisitor: Rise of the Red Blade
Disney Mirrorverse: Pure of Heart
The Minecraft Mob Squad Series

THE SHADOW SERIES,
WRITTEN AS LILA BOWEN
Wake of Vultures
Conspiracy of Ravens
Malice of Crows
Treason of Hawks

GUILLOTINE

DELILAH S.
DAWSON

TITAN BOOKS

Guillotine
Print edition ISBN: 9781803368337
E-book edition ISBN: 9781803368344

Published by Titan Books
A division of Titan Publishing Group Ltd
144 Southwark Street, London SE1 0UP
www.titanbooks.com

First edition: September 2024
10 9 8 7 6 5 4 3 2 1

A CIP catalogue record for this title is
available from the British Library.

Printed and bound by
CPI Group (UK) Ltd, Croydon, CR0 4YY.

If you've ever cleaned someone else's dirty toilet…

If you've ever been cussed out while working a cash register…

If you've ever gotten covered in restaurant trash juice…

This one's for you.

You deserve a lot more than a book.

CONTENT WARNING

In this book, bad people get what they deserve, and they deserve
what they get. There are many unsettling deaths, which I found
quite cathartic to write. My publisher has identified the following
trigger warnings:

Gore
Graphic depictions of injury
Sexual assault (off-page)
Incest (off-page)
Forced pregnancy (off-page)
Rape (off-page)
Abortion (off-page)

While I have never been in a position similar to Dez, I lived
through childhood sexual assault, domestic violence, stalking,
and rape. When I write about these topics, I do so through the lens
of a survivor's rage. I have also been locked in a toy chest, and I
will hold that grudge until I die.

If you're still in, I sincerely hope you enjoy my little murder book.
I very much enjoyed writing it.

1

There is a certain languor in some kinds of work, a pleasant and soporific monotony that quiets the mind and allows it to tune in to an age-old frequency, the timeless buzz of worker bees happily humming. For Dez Lane, 21, this pleasure settles over her whenever she's sewing things by hand. Today, she's replacing beads on a flapper dress, bent over her worktable and wearing granny glasses on a long chain, her fingers sore from the intricate and repetitive motions. This dress is part of her senior thesis in Fashion Design, and it has to be perfect.

As she carefully pins down each bead in the fragile old fabric, her mind roams like a bird's wings skimming over a field and alights on a freshman year lecture with Dr. Bartz. That was the day she learned about the history of beads — that the oldest beads on record have been around for over a hundred thousand years. Cavemen drilled holes in snail shells and fished bits of mother-of-pearl out of the sea. Egyptians turned crushed quartz into faience tubes and draped glittering nets over their dead. Ancient eyes alit on flashing beetle wings and stones, and something deep in their hearts told them, "I want that."

And that's what Dez loves about fashion — when she sees some beautiful object, and it clicks into place like the safety harness on a roller coaster, and she thinks, *I want that, I need that, I must use that to make something transcendent.* She craves this feeling enough to build her future around it, to stake all her hopes on it. She's going to be a designer with her own house one day, making dresses for the red carpet and pinning swaths of cloth around the surgically enhanced hips of the world's most glamorous women. She is ambitious, and she will do anything to make her dreams come true. Her mother is counting on her, and once she leaves SCAD, there will be no more scholarships, no more free student housing. One more month, and her entire life is sink or swim.

And that is why this dress must be perfect.

Her phone buzzes, and she uncurls her hunched spine and stretches, moving her massive braid of curly apricot-colored hair to her other shoulder. As soon as she unlocks her phone, her heart jerks in her chest.

This is the email she's been waiting for —

The one that could change everything.

Dear Desirée Lane, the email begins. *We regret to inform you —*

And that's when Dez stops reading.

There is no coming back from *We regret to inform you.*

If there was any good news at all, any hope, they would've led with that.

At least they responded. Most of the jobs she's applied for don't even bother with that basic kindness. She wakes up her laptop and pulls up her spreadsheet, clicking the Nope box and filing that dead end away where she can't see it. The list of possibilities is dwindling. It's apparently impossible to land an interview at a major fashion house if you're a broke nobody in Savannah, Georgia, with zero connections.

If only this was the eighties, back when any girl with a side pony could land a job at *Sassy* magazine by writing her resume on a pair of acid-washed jeans.

Her mother warned her, told her to get a degree in something real that would pay the bills and enjoy fashion on her own time, but Dez would rather die than be a CPA and live a life bounded by numbers. She loves color, excess, feathers, beads, sequins. It's all her mom's fault. She used to bring home the forgotten things she found cleaning hotel rooms at the Cosmopolitan in Vegas, and the first time tiny Dez got her hands on a pint-sized pageant gown, it was *Game Over* for a khaki kind of life.

The happy hum of hand-sewing has turned into the glaring pain of silence, and Dez stares at her spreadsheet. She's too smart to feel this lost, too resourceful to have so few options. If she can't get a job in high fashion in the traditional way, she has to move sideways. That's what you do when you grew up poor: You think outside the box.

There's one avenue she hasn't fully explored because...

Well, because she's too proud. And because she knows it won't be fun.

But it's been sitting in the back of her mind, waiting like a wad of grimy twenties under the mattress for a moment of true desperation.

With a determined exhale, she scrolls through her phone contacts until she gets to Patrick Ruskin Yucky Yucky Ick Ick Ick. There's just one message. Although everyone at school knows him or knows of him, Dez met Patrick for the first time at a bar last week. He slid the phone from her unwilling hand and texted himself so that he'd have her number, and she was too surprised to stop him. She danced with her girlfriends until she forgot about this transgression, and the next day he sent one missive.

Let me take you out and spoil you. I'll be good, I promise.

The fact that he texts with full grammar and punctuation is not the only thing that makes Patrick abhorrent. He's arrogant, judgmental, sexist, and worst of all, doesn't know how to take no for an answer, hence that last text. But there are two things about Patrick that might be handy for Dez's situation. For one thing, he's rich. For another thing, his mother is Marie Caulfield-Ruskin, editor-in-chief of *Nouveau* magazine, one of the only fashion magazines still standing — and thriving. *Nouveau* makes waifs into It girls, struggling writers into columnists, unknown designers into household names. *Nouveau* is the reigning queen of fashion, an outlier, an anomaly, a golden ziggurat lording it over a sea of once-proud magazines that have now become fly-by-night infotainment websites.

And Dez wants a piece of that pyramid, just one gold brick.

So what if Patrick grabbed her butt at that bar? And so what if he basically forced her to give him her number? So what if he caught her elbow hard enough to bruise, just so she had to stop and talk to him on the way to the bathroom?

All she has to do is fend him off long enough to get an in with his mom. She can blink her fake eyelashes at him and laugh at his jokes and dress up in her slinkiest dresses and stuff herself with crab at the nicest restaurants in the city and make him fall in love with her. Women have done worse for less return on investment. It's the way of the world.

Aw, that's sweet, she texts back. *What did you have in mind?*

She's not surprised when he responds with, *Who is this?*

Dez from the bar. Long red hair, short silver dress?

She chooses the things she thinks he's most likely to remember.

After a moment, he texts back.

Elizabeth's, 7pm tonight. Where do I pick you up?

Dez grins. He's so easy.

She doesn't want him to know she's a scholarship kid still in free student housing as a senior, so she gives him the address of her favorite Victorian downtown.

See you there, he responds, plus a winky face.

She goes to her closet and flips through her dresses. Some she made by hand, some she thrifted and altered, a few she found off the clearance rack and fixed up. It's pathetic, how scared most shoppers are of a missing button, loose thread, or deodorant skid mark, but Dez loves the thrill of the hunt. Anyone with money can buy something perfect, but there's a shine to stolen glamour that someone with a black credit card will never understand. There's a magic to taking something no one else wants and making it something everyone praises.

As she gets dressed that night and does her makeup, she is well aware that she is baiting a hook, choosing just the right fly, the right feathers, the right — whatever Will was doing on *Hannibal*, back when he had encephalitis and went fishing a lot. Her goal is to make Patrick Ruskin fall in love with her. She can't be seen as a fling; it has to feel real if she wants in with his family. She will do anything to avoid returning home to Las Vegas, to the couch of her mom's cramped one-bedroom apartment, to the smog-filled air and breath-stealing desert. She did not come this far, follow her hopes across the country and get her dream degree, just to end up cleaning hotel rooms at the Cosmopolitan and watching her exhausted, overworked, under-insured mom wince every time she bends down to pick up a discarded champagne bottle in a room that costs her entire weekly salary for one night.

She chooses an emerald-green dress, halfway between sexy and classy, and lets her long, wild hair tumble to her waist in a cascade of curls it's taken her years to master. She knows just the right accessories to set off her beauty, to bring out the seafoam in her blue-green eyes and the unexpectedly golden tones in her skin. She has never known her father, has no idea who he is or what he looks like, but she has been told all her life that she looks exotic, like a little doll, and asked what she is and where she's from, like she's some weird breed of dog. She finishes her outfit with her beloved pair of thrifted Jimmy Choos, which she keeps immaculate, the leather always touched up carefully, and an antique purse that she prizes more than any name brand.

When Patrick pulls up to the address she's given him at 7:15, she steps from the shadows, smiling, welcoming.

The moment she's in his black Tesla, his hand is on her knee, a heavy gold ring with a family crest shining on his knuckle, and she swallows down her distaste and tells herself that every relationship is, in its way, transactional. From what she's heard of Patrick, he really only wants one thing, and she is happy to provide that thing, and thus perhaps they can trade. She has found something shiny, and she tells herself, "I want that." Maybe it's not Patrick Ruskin, but it's what he represents. It's the doors he can open. Much like a dress on the clearance rack, for the sake of her future, she'll take what she finds — what's within reach — and make it work.

2

On their first date, Patrick does all the talking, and Dez pretends to hang on his every word. They eat a seven-course prix fixe meal at the nicest restaurant in Savannah with wine pairings, and it would be the best night of her life if she didn't have to put up with his embarrassing behavior. He's rude to the waitstaff, and when he tries to play footsie with her, she jerks away and drops her fork because she's fairly certain he's dented her shin. At the end of the date, she tilts her face up toward him outside a building in which she dreams of living, and he rams his tongue down her throat with all the passion and elegance of a clumsy dog sticking its snout in a jar of peanut butter.

This is not a man who's ever given a single second of consideration to another person's pleasure. He's never had to. He can have anything he wants. Money tends to do that.

On their second date, he takes her to a loud party in the penthouse of a fancy hotel, steering her around the many rooms of the suite with a protective arm around her waist, taking every chance to use the top of her ass as a handlebar. He brings her glass after glass of champagne, introduces her to a fleet of men who look and dress and act just like him, and their eyes roam hungrily over her body as though she's a boat they'd like to take for an aggressive spin before buying. No one asks her about herself, her major or her past or her future. She is an object, but a beautiful one. It's almost a relief when they forget her to argue over football.

On their third date, Patrick orders oysters, slurping the gooey gray blobs from their dinosaur shells while making intense eye contact; he doesn't seem to understand that oysters are only an aphrodisiac to the person who eats them, and he doesn't offer a single one to Dez. By the time they pull up to his apartment building, his stomach is making terrible noises, and he pushes her hand off his thigh. On the way up in the elevator, he stares off into space as if troubled by a noise only he can hear. Dez spends the next two hours rubbing his back and murmuring sweetly as he hurls into one of those fancy Japanese toilets that can sing a lullaby while heating your tushy. She brings him ice water, tuts over him like a nursemaid, and kindly ignores the fact that he has obviously shit his slacks. She doesn't leave until the worst is over and he's showered and tucked up in a bed bigger than her dorm room, sweating through his navy silk sheets.

After she kisses him gently on the forehead, he reaches for her hand.

"Tonight didn't go as planned," he croaks.

"Poor baby," she says. "Let me know if you need me."

When he texts her the next day asking for ginger ale and Saltines, she magically appears in his apartment to make toast and heat up soup and coo over what a rough night he had. He doesn't thank her, but he does say she'd make a good nurse. The lust is back in his eyes again, so he must be feeling better. When he jams his tongue down her throat, she is certain she tastes the sea.

On their fourth date, they go on a carriage ride downtown, which isn't as romantic as it seems unless you're really into the smell of manure and the ramblings of an old man dressed like a pirate who is more interested in pointing out ghost sightings than in letting a couple canoodle. Dez is grateful to the pirate; she doesn't want Patrick pawing at her in front of the tourists, with her crotch at eyeball height. At least they're not eating spoiled seafood this time, she tells herself.

In the car on the way back to the place he thinks is her home, his firm fingers roam so far up the hem of her tight dress that his clunky ring catches on the fabric. When he yanks it free, they both hear the cloth rip.

"I'll have my mother's people send something over," Patrick says in what should be an apology but isn't. "Just text me your size later." The hand goes right back to business, but the dress is too tight to give him much room to maneuver up her thigh while driving the narrow, cobbled streets.

"Are you going to invite me in?" he says, car idling.

Dez blushes and looks down, feigning shyness and modesty that she doesn't actually feel. "It's only our fifth date," she tells him. "And my place is a mess. I wasn't sure what to wear and had to try everything on to get it right."

He's disappointed, but Dez knows that if she gives him what he wants now, he'll discard her like an old toy. He leans over to kiss her, and he tastes of beer and barbecue sliders and the certainty that even if she seems out of reach now, nothing ever eludes him for long. She returns the kiss as best she can, allows his hand to roam over her chest, but pulls away a bit as it slips inside her dress.

"I'm going away for Easter," he tells her, sensually wiping his thumb over her upper lip like something he saw in a porno once. "My family does a big thing every year at the beach house. So I won't be around for a week or so."

When Dez gasps, it's very real, but it's not because she's on fire to see him again. It's because where his family goes, his mother will be.

"You have a beach house? That's so *romantic*," she breathes, chest heaving prettily. "Is it nearby?"

A car honks behind them, and Patrick looks back over his shoulder with annoyance but doesn't move the car. "Yeah, on a private island south of Tybee. My family's been there for generations. It's where I grew up. We spend the summer there. Holidays, too."

"It sounds gorgeous." She turns toward him, giving his hand just a little more space to creep up her short dress. "I've never been to the beach. Can you believe that? Four years here, and it just somehow never happened. I bet I would love the ocean."

Patrick's nose flares like a predator scenting prey. He's handsome — there's no question about that, with his thick, perfectly tousled, sandy hair, and his soulful blue-gray eyes under expressive eyebrows. He's tall enough, fit, strong, and well on his way to a future as a cinematographer, which probably means he just wants free rein to bang actresses and yell at the crew. People like him get to become whatever they want. But he's not particularly clever, and he's definitely not creative. If he's ever been played before, Dez thinks, he wasn't aware of it. He probably believes every woman he encounters is lucky to be with him — or a frigid prude if she turns down his advances.

"I mean, I haven't used my bikini this whole time. Not even a pool." She moves her hair back, revealing the curve of her neck and bare shoulder. His eyes twitch back and forth like a cat following the movement of prey.

"You could join me," he finally says. "I have my own suite. But..." He pauses, and she pouts, sticking out her lower lip. "Some things are just for the family, you know? You wouldn't be invited to some of the events. Like, Easter morning croquet is just for us. And brunch on the yacht. But whenever I'm busy, you could lay out by the pool, work on your tan. My brothers bring their wives."

Her response is not acting; she really is ecstatic. "Oh, my God, Patrick, really? That would be like a dream come true! I would love to!" She leans in and kisses him on the cheek, one hand on his shoulder, one on his thigh. He hums to himself, satisfied, and pulls into the nearest dark alley, where he unbuckles and resettles himself, spreading his knees as far as the car will allow.

Dez flicks her long hair to the side, letting it cascade over his lap as she leans down. She decided a long time ago that she would do anything to make her dreams come true and escape her mother's reality, and at least he finishes quickly.

3

When Patrick picks her up for the trip, Dez is dressed like a screen siren, her lips painted bright matte red, her cat-eye sunglasses down, and a scarf jauntily tied around her hair. She spent far too much time choosing what to wear, knowing that she has to make an immediate positive impact on Marie Caulfield-Ruskin. She's wearing a vintage gingham dress she expertly rehabilitated, redesigned, and tailored to her measurements, plus wedge sandals with a wicker purse, and her suitcase is a stunning leather relic from the fifties, the sort of thing they just don't make anymore. She looks like Barbie, if Barbie was five-foot-three and had curly strawberry blond hair.

"We could pull over first," Patrick says after stowing her bags in the trunk and looking her up and down. He really is like a dog: generally in a good mood, assumes everyone loves him, has a one-track mind centered on his own selfish hunger that assumes he has a right to whatever he finds, becomes suddenly cruel when provoked. He inclines his head toward his favorite alley.

"I can't meet your family after doing... that." She playfully slaps his shoulder.

They've had three more dates, and they still haven't actually had sex, but Dez knows how to keep him coming back for more. It doesn't take much work, at least; he's a simple man and not overendowed. As someone accustomed to unpleasant labor, she's able to compartmentalize and uses that time to plan her outfits for the week. On their last date, he brought her a garment bag, and the dress inside was couture, a sample from Prada with one picked thread, now her prized possession. She brought it along for the trip — after making a few adjustments. Patrick is disappointing in many ways, but at least he's a man of his word. He can tear as many of her dresses as he likes with his gaudy ring, if this is how he makes up for it.

"Then maybe you can do that after meeting my family," he says, waggling his eyebrows with the optimism of a golden retriever.

He pulls into traffic and navigates out of downtown, and Dez settles back and watches the scenery. Once they're out on the open road, she asks, "So tell me about your family. What should I expect?"

She has already done an internet search on every relative she could find online, but she wants him to think that she is an innocent, sexy idiot. She is curious to see who will be there, and what he'll say about them. The Ruskins only seem to have sons, and even then, they don't all marry, so it's mostly men and their successful trophy wives. There was no information whatsoever on the family home they'll be visiting, and that, too, is curious. Aren't most families proud of their palatial estates?

"Well, Mother and Father will be there, of course," he says, weaving in and out of traffic. "Grandfather and Grandmother live there all the time, and the uncles will be there. My oldest brother William works in finance and philanthropy, and then my brother Anthony works with Mother at the magazine, in the accounting department."

She nods. "Does your family get along?"

He glances at her like this is an odd question. "As well as anyone can. When you're part of this sort of dynasty, you're taught certain rules from an early age, and you either toe the line or you get..." He pauses, searching for the word. "Not just disinherited but kicked out of the family. It happened to my brother Luke, and he basically disappeared. Haven't seen him for two years." He looks at her so long that she is suddenly terrified they'll be in an accident, but then she notices that the Tesla is in self-driving mode, not that it makes her feel any safer.

"You'll have to sign a non-disclosure agreement to enter the property," he tells her. "I hope that won't be a problem."

Her teeth briefly grind as she smiles. "Of course not. That makes total sense."

Dez hasn't been this far out of Savannah; she wasn't lying about never seeing the beach. The claustrophobic streets of downtown have given way to a highway she didn't even know existed, rising up over the swamp and driving directly into the sky. She wishes he had a convertible for this part of the journey so that she could feel some true measure of joy, some moment of infinite possibility and abandon. Instead, bounded by the smooth, impersonal lines of a space-age car and breathing in recycled air mixed with his breath, she is all too aware that every part of this experience is a construct. A construct that serves her, certainly, but she wishes for a life that allowed for more authenticity. She's never had a long-term boyfriend, never found a comfortable happiness that she could live with. She's too focused on her work, on her dream. And too unwilling to settle for anything less than perfection. There is nothing she would rather do on a Friday night than listen to old Tori Amos records while hemming a sleeve, and most guys only find that adorable and quirky for the first few weeks. She was only in the bar where Patrick borderline assaulted her because she was hoping to net some contacts from a returning alumnus after a lecture.

"You're mad because I want to take you out to dinner? I'm your boyfriend. I should be your priority," Eli told her once, when he'd randomly shown up at her door. He wanted to be an Imagineer and already had a good start because he lived in a world of pure imagination, especially regarding his own genius.

"Then make scheduling your priority. You never actually asked me out. I'm not a vending machine," she snapped. "Or your wife. We've been dating for a month. I'm not going to sit here in power saver mode for when you actually put down the bong and want to do something."

He went out that night and didn't come back. She doesn't miss him.

The Tesla smoothly decelerates around a curve. They're off the highway and on a long, low, two-lane road through a marsh now. The afternoon sun sparks off the brackish water among the golden-yellow stalks of sea grass, birds wheeling and diving and crying overhead like they've lost something precious. Among the reeds, Dez sees men on little skiffs, pulling up crab traps and casting out lines. Their boats are so small it almost looks like they're standing on the water, an entire herd of Jesuses.

Or would it be Jesii?

"It's not too far," Patrick says. "The island is out past Skidaway. It's not on the maps."

"What's it called?"

He looks at her again, amused. "If you don't want something to be findable, you don't name it. We just call it the Island."

Although he's never turned on the radio before, he does so now, just a little louder than it should be. Bon Iver blares, adding a funereal feeling to the endless marshes. Dez has a million more questions, but she doesn't want to push Patrick. He doesn't seem like the kind of guy who has a lot of patience once things aren't going exactly how he wants them. If he realizes he's being interrogated, he might sense that she's not just here because she loves being face-down in his lap. He can still turn around and take her back. Or worse, just dump her here on the side of the road, a few feet from the stinking marsh. She can imagine herself standing there under the pounding spring sun, her toes covered in sand, frantically trying to call an Uber as seagulls dive-bomb her like Tippi Hedren in *The Birds*.

After a long time and a switch to Kanye, they enter a national park. Patrick waves to the guy at the guard station but doesn't stop to pay the fee. He goes exactly the speed limit, his freshly washed Tesla at odds with the dusty, kayak-laden station wagons and converted camper vans parked under the spreading oaks.

Patrick turns down a dirt road labeled *Maintenance – Park Personnel only*, and Dez knows better than to ask what he's doing. She can tell by his smug grin, by his arm draped behind her seat, that he knows exactly where he's going and is pleased by the seeming impudence, like he's getting away with something. For a dirt road through a forest, the way is surprisingly smooth, the branches and brush cut back to ensure not a single scraping twig touches his car — or a car even bigger than his.

After what feels like miles, the trees fall away to reveal a tiny, paved parking lot shaded with solar panels and filled with vehicles that make Dez understand exactly why the maintenance road was pristine. A giant black SUV limo sits beside a neon green Bugatti and a sleek silver Rolls, the only cars she can readily identify on her own. Patrick's Tesla is the least impressive of what she sees, and she knows it's top of the line. He pulls into an open spot and gets out of the car, stretching as if he's been driving all day instead of maybe forty-five minutes. Dez gets out, too, and is immediately struck by the absolute freshness of the air.

So this is why people come to the ocean, she thinks. *It's like drinking water when you don't even know you're thirsty.*

She turns to face the waves lapping up against the rocky shore. On a government-run island on the other side of a dirt road, she would expect a ratty little pier and an old dinghy, but no expense has been spared here. The waiting dock is large, clean, and looks like it was built yesterday. The waiting ship is what she would consider a yacht, and yet she suspects Patrick thinks of it like a tub toy. Beyond the dock, the air grows hazy, but she can see an island there, inviting as a mirage.

White sand, inexplicably green landscaping, and a home so large and sprawling that it seems like a city on its own. Like a pink castle built to blend in with the rosiest of dawns. A high-pitched whinny pierces the air.

"Horses?" she asks, turning to Patrick, unable to hide her delight.

She has always secretly harbored hopes of being a horse girl, but being poor and living in a desert kills such dreams rather quickly.

"Polo ponies," he corrects, as if this is the least interesting thing about the island. "My grandparents both played. All of us have to, or there aren't enough people for a proper game."

He pops the trunk, and a man in a light pink uniform of crisp pink polo and crisper pink khakis materializes to help with their bags. Patrick has only brought a gray Goyard duffle, and the man slings it over a shoulder and takes Dez's suitcase. He doesn't speak to them, keeps his face turned away and his sunglasses firmly in place, inviting them to pretend that he doesn't exist. As he jogs toward the waiting boat, Patrick takes his time, reaching for Dez's hand. There is something strangely ceremonial about their path, walking toward the grand boat that will take them to an even larger house. Dez does not like Patrick — he is essentially unlikeable. She likes the way his money and connections can open doors that she can't open on her own. But she likes this moment. It feels grander than life, as if she's accidentally stepped into the sort of movie they just don't make anymore. This doesn't feel like some weekend jaunt. It feels... big. Important. As if something is beginning.

"I hope they like me," she murmurs. "Your family."

Patrick doesn't break his stride, doesn't even squeeze her hand in reassurance. "Oh, don't worry. They don't like anybody. It doesn't matter, in the long run."

Dez does not find this comforting.

He releases her hand at the dock and motions for her to go first. Dez walks up the ramp and onto the boat, nearly turning her ankle in her high wedges. She definitely brought the wrong shoes, but he never said anything about a boat, and she just assumed you could drive onto the island, like Tybee or Jekyll. She's never been on a boat before. It swoops and rocks uneasily underneath her, and she's grateful the moment Patrick indicates she should take a seat.

They're outside on a sort of bench, and the moment they're settled, another man in an identical pink uniform brings them glass flutes of champagne. Dez thanks him but Patrick doesn't. She watches the man as he crosses the boat. His pink shirt, shorts, and socks are all precisely the same hue, the exact color of a kitten's nose, the fabrics perfectly cut and unblemished. His shoes are an unobtrusive grayish brown, their pink soles grippy, a concession, she supposes, to working on a slippery boat. His aviator sunglasses are tinted rose gold, their mirrors hiding his eyes. His hair is brown, short, and slicked down. She would not be able to pick him out of a lineup and isn't even certain if he's the same man who took their bags.

Other than the man in pink, they are utterly alone.

Engines churn, and the boat begins to move with the slow power of a monster waking from sleep. Mist fills the air, dancing with rainbows, as they amble toward the castle in the clouds.

4

The castle slips in and out of vision; it's as if mist shimmies along the water, coquettishly hiding the island and revealing it like a burlesque dancer's feathered fans. Dez wants to ask questions, but again, she feels as if they would be unwelcome. Patrick wants silence, and he expects her to accept that. It almost feels like a test. She isn't sure if he's smart enough to make it a test, but she knows her job, so she remains silent as she sips the champagne. Bubbles make it easier to pretend.

The boat seems too big for the crossing, and she wonders that it doesn't run aground, but the trip is smooth and short. Whoever is driving expertly pulls up alongside an identical dock. She would expect to find speedboats and jet skis and possibly even a banana boat for the younger cousins moored here, maybe a rack of paddleboards and kayaks for a serene morning float, but the dock is immaculately kept and empty. Not even a rowboat or one of those circular life savers. There is no beach, just the same rocky ledge, the water crashing against it. If she managed to fall over the edge — perhaps a ten-foot drop — she suspects she would be smashed to bits against the wall by the impersonal, ancient rage of these deep blue waters.

As Dez disembarks, she can see that the wall isn't actually rock — it's seashells. Layer upon layer of crusty gray shells, thick as ramparts, keen as knives, surrounding the island and disappearing into the water below.

"What are those?" she asks Patrick, breaking the odd silence.

He glances down. "Oysters. They just build on each other. Watch out, though — they're really sharp."

Dez has only seen oysters on that one terrible date with him, and she recognizes them now, sort of. Odd that something so jagged and rough in the wild could be so slimy and valuable on the inside once domesticated. Or perhaps they're raised in laboratories, planted in rows like corn. Dez knows nothing of oyster life, and all her pearls are fakes that have to be replaced when the dust begins to rub off the plain white plastic.

The man in pink carries their bags up a white shell path toward the castle. Each step brings a dusty crunch, and when she looks down, she sees lacy ridges and Fibonacci swirls and delicate, elfin curves like little mouse ears, the shells bleached white and broken to crumbs, ghosts of the living oysters in the sea. Instead of a beach, there is intricate landscaping set off by the snowy white lines of crisscrossing avenues. Dark green hedges, pink stucco walls, and heavy wood gates divide up the space, while pretty flowers and bushes distract the eye. Whoever planned this place was precise, and whoever keeps it up must carry a T-square around in their pocket to make sure none of the tiny shells dare go astray.

They pass an elegant croquet field with wickets in pink, white, and lavender and emerge beside a luxurious pool. Dez is stunned by the sparkling blue grotto, waterfall, and multiple hot tubs, each hidden by natural-looking stacks and caves of stone. Fire pits and sitting areas sprawl around in private corners fanned by palm trees. An outdoor kitchen sits under a pergola overtaken by fuchsia bougainvillea, complete with a massive adobe pizza oven, a butcher block counter, a sink, a grill and — Jesus, an entire outdoor refrigerator nicer than any fridge she's ever owned, the kind with a freezer drawer on the bottom and a computer in case you forget if you have milk.

Other than the man in pink, Dez hasn't seen another person. No one lounges by the pool or waves at her with a croquet mallet in hand. When she looks back to the dock, the ship has disappeared. There must be another dock somewhere more convenient, she reasons. Surely there is some sandy white beach among the dunes. Why own an island if you're not going to enjoy the ocean?

A flash of pink catches her eye, and she sees a woman walking the paths closer to the house. Like the men, she's in all pink, her dress plain and full and starched, down to her calves, with a pink kerchief covering her hair. Dez's perspective shifts, and the woman disappears against the walls of the castle — house — building? Patrick's family apparently decided to go all-in on this exact shade of pink.

They're near the estate now, approaching a big courtyard that was made for events. A pink fountain in the center sends water playfully splashing upward with a pleasant tinkling noise. In another world, this would be the circular drive full of cars, but Dez hasn't seen a single vehicle here, not even a golf cart. A man sits on the edge of the fountain, smoking a cigarette. He's in all white, looking like he walked out of a Rock Hudson movie. Dez knows who he is, of course, but no one else needs to know that.

"Patrick," the man says, standing up and holding his cigarette to the side.

"Father."

Patrick steps up, and they share the coldest embrace Dez has ever seen, like two wooden puppets forced together. She doesn't get the idea that they dislike each other, just that touching is some forced concession for her sake and not something they've ever naturally done. Internally, she shivers. Maybe she grew up dirt poor, but her mother's hugs were always full of very real love.

"And this must be Desirée. Welcome to the Island. I'm Bill." Patrick's father holds out his arms, and Dez has no choice but to endure a much more personal hug, the kind that makes her feel like a piece of meat being tested for doneness. He smells of cigarettes and wood and alcohol and some very expensive cologne that's supposed to cover up all the bad smells but doesn't, because her nose is as sharp as her eyes.

"Nice to meet you," she says, stepping back to Patrick's side and grateful, for once, to be there. "Thank you so much for inviting me along. It's absolutely beautiful here."

Bill half turns to look up at the — well, Dez is just going to think of it as *the castle*, because it makes the word *house* sound woefully ineffectual. Its three floors of windows gleam in the slanting sun. "I can't take much credit for it, but we're glad you could join us. Marie looks forward to meeting you at dinner, but she's holed up with Anthony doing spreadsheets at the moment." He shakes his head like running the world's foremost fashion magazine is a frivolous hobby. Dez notices that his way of speaking is almost surgical in its precision — probably a side effect of being a state judge.

"Where's everyone else?" Patrick asks.

Bill sits back on the fountain, takes a drag of his cigarette. "William is at the stables with Grandmother to see the new foal. Christiane and the boy are at the other pool with Genevieve and her brood." He rolls his eyes as if baffled that anyone might wish to enjoy a luxurious private pool. "Grandfather and Frank are at the courts, waiting for me to finish my horrible little habit here." He holds up his cigarette, takes a drag with his eyes closed as if it's the only joy left in the world, and then stubs it out on the ground, leaving a black streak. "Once all the paperwork is done, you're welcome to join us. I need a partner." He looks to Dez, skeptical. "Do you play?"

"Tennis? I'm afraid not. I've always wanted to learn, but I would most likely just ruin an actual game."

He nods. "Well then. There are two pools. This one will be quiet, but you might as well get to know the wives."

"I look forward to it."

He stands. "As do we all. And again, welcome."

Dez wonders if he knows what the word welcome actually means, because this is not it. "Thank you so much."

He points at Patrick. "Paperwork, then tennis." With that, William Ruskin III gives her a sharp, studying look and departs. He's in his late fifties but looks thirty-five, and she can see exactly what Patrick will look like in thirty years.

"Paperwork," Patrick repeats, as if the very thought is exhausting. "Although the good news is that you only have to sign it once. It will cover all future interactions with the family. Might as well get it over with so we can get you into that bikini."

The man in pink has disappeared with their bags, so she takes Patrick's waiting hand and lets him lead her into the grand, open doors of the castle. They're in a soaring white marble foyer, every surface gleaming. It's both empty and opulent, as cold and inhospitable as a glacier, their footsteps echoing. Patrick guides her into a study, the kind of sumptuously impersonal office staged in luxury real estate photos where no one has ever done a lick of actual work. Two leather club chairs laze before the delicate glass desk, on which sits a stapled stack of papers and a heavy metal pen.

"Read it and sign it where indicated," Patrick says with no warmth whatsoever. "If you choose not to sign it, you'll be escorted off the Island. I'll be staying here, but we'll have someone meet you at the dock and get you back home." He gives her a look she hasn't seen before. His eyes are gray today, hard as stone, his lips unsmiling. "Back home to your dorm, I mean. Not that Victorian you always want to meet at, for some reason."

A lead ball drops in Dez's stomach. How long has he known about that? Why hasn't he said anything?

And then it hits her.

If they're making her sign all these papers, they've likely researched her to make sure Patrick isn't bringing home someone dangerous. She did online searches on them, but the Ruskins must have someone on staff who does this for a living, a private investigator charged with keeping the family safe from charlatans. They probably know her bank account balance down to the cent, her grades, her pap smear history.

In this moment, it occurs to her that she was so desperate, and she thought herself so clever, that she didn't really think through all the realities of this plan. She forgot that even if Patrick is a fool, the Ruskins as a whole are not.

"Seems fair," she says, keeping her voice even.

"I'm going to get changed for tennis. When you're done signing, someone will take you to your room. All good?"

He seems back to his sunny self, maybe even a little nervous. She likes him better this way.

"All good. Thanks." She turns to the papers and takes up the pen.

"And Dez?" he says from the door.

She looks up. "Yes?"

"If my dad ever tells you to do something, it's not just a suggestion." Winking at her like he's fulfilled his responsibilities and is finally free, he leaves.

Dez has never yet lived a life where she followed a man's commands, but she's spent enough time in hotels to understand how to be an excellent guest. She certainly doesn't want to embarrass herself in front of the elder Ruskins, and especially not in front of the husband of Marie Caulfield-Ruskin. She turns back to the paperwork.

The typed letters are tiny, the contract's complicated legalese impossible to tease apart. It might as well be in a different language. There are multiple places for her to initial and sign, all marked with little pink tabs. They have her full name and real address, her mother's name and address. One page is marked with the biggest tab of all, a bright red one.

READ THIS PAGE BEFORE SIGNING, it says.

She turns to the page, almost relieved to find a simple numbered list in a reasonably sized font, preceded by a single paragraph.

This list hereby condenses the non-disclosure agreement between GUEST and THE RUSKIN TRUST. As we understand that full legal documentation can prove cumbersome and confusing, you will be asked to initial each term to ensure you are familiar with what you are signing.

1. *You will relinquish all cell phones, cameras, computers, tablets, video game consoles, microphones, recorders, and electronic devices, including wearables and exercise trackers. You will be searched, as will your luggage. Glucose monitors are the only exception. Visitors discovered harboring unreported technology will be immediately removed and permanently banned.*

Dez grimaces. No Fancy Pink Island Castle poolside selfies, then.

2. *By signing, you acknowledge that there is no wifi or cell phone service on the Island. The Island can be accessed by boat only. Immediate medical treatment is not insured. You participate in Island life at your own risk.*

But surely rich people can get a helicopter here, if there's an actual problem? Surely they *own* a helicopter?

3. *By signing, you acknowledge that you will not speak of anything you see or hear on the Island once you return to the mainland. For all intents and purposes, the Island does not exist. This gag order in perpetuity includes not only the press, the police, and the courts, but friends and family and any future creative endeavors, including anything published anonymously. Failure to retain your silence on this topic makes you immediately subject to the harshest penalties possible to the full extent of the law and including full financial damages.*

So much for using this experience in her next cover letter. *I Went to the Private Island of Marie Caulfield-Ruskin, and All I Got Was This Stupid Pink Shirt.*

4. *The Island is made possible by our loyal staff, who are well trained and extremely well compensated. Please do not interfere with Island staff business. We must insist that our*

guests do not attempt to fraternize with the Island staff in
any way. Island staff are expected to be rarely seen and never
heard, and they take great pride in their work. Guests seen
harassing Island staff will be removed. Staff members can be
easily identified by their trademark pink uniforms. Staff areas
are well marked and off limits to guests. Island staff are well
versed in this regard, and they WILL report you.

Ah. No wonder the pink man didn't speak. He's apparently not allowed to.

5. *Guests can be removed at any time and for any reason, at*
   the discretion of the owners and staff of the Island. If so
   removed, this non-disclosure agreement will remain in place
   in perpetuity. Guests are heavily cautioned not to attempt
   to break this agreement in retaliation. Assume we know
   everything.

And then there's a line to sign and date, as if this is all perfectly normal.

Dez holds the pen, staring at that blank line.

This NDA is, frankly, terrifying.

And insane.

She is signing away every human right she has while standing on this island.

If Patrick — or anyone — hurts her, she can't report it to the police.

If she's hurt, she can't count on her insurance to cover it.

She doesn't even have the simple pleasure of bragging that she's been here.

And yet...

If she doesn't sign it, some anonymous and silent man in pink will drag her across the sea, taxi her to her dorm, and dump her with her beautiful suitcase and her dignity, and she will never know what might have been. She will probably be blackballed from *Nouveau* — and anywhere else where fashion is still valued.

She doesn't read the more impenetrable pages.

She initials every spot and signs on the big line with all her usual flourishes.

If she plays it right on this island, that signature will actually be worth something one day.

5

As soon as the ink is dry, a large man in pink appears to silently claim the stapled papers and the pen. He's not in the polo and shorts, though — he's in an actual suit. Jacket, tie, shirt, slacks, all in a shade of pink that is becoming slightly overwhelming, like chugging an entire metaphorical bottle of Pepto Bismol. He looks just like all the others, but an exceptionally sturdy forty-five. His smile does not reach his eyes.

"I'm Mr. Rose, the butler. Did you have any questions?"

"So many! This place is fascinating. When was it built — "

"I apologize for the confusion. Did you have any questions about the paperwork?"

It's a question, but with an inflection that suggests she should not, in fact, have any questions. Dez has never encountered someone so simultaneously rude and polite, and she is thrown off. She does not have a script for this kind of social interaction. She instinctually dislikes Mr. Rose and wants to get away from him as soon as possible.

"No questions," she says, because she knows that's what he wants her to say.

"Excellent. Follow me, please, Miss Lane."

She wants to ask him his first name, if he really is well compensated, if he likes working here, because she's heard her mother's stories about cleaning up after the absurdly rich. But he carries himself like he has power, and she doesn't want to get tossed out before she's even seen the upstairs, and the paperwork was very explicit about this sort of thing. Mr. Rose looks fit and put together, perfect posture, beefy, tan, and efficient, so she has to assume that if he wasn't happy here, he'd go somewhere else.

He leads her up the grand staircase to the second floor, which offers a long, pale pink hallway and heavy wood doors at intervals that suggest these are not just bedrooms but the suites she heard Patrick mention. Between the doors are yellowing family portraits with cracked varnish, newer paintings of various roses, and ancient-looking tables that hold elegant vases overflowing with all-white flower arrangements. Farther on, they turn a corner, and the doors here are spaced more regularly and with less artwork, the hallway more straightforward and utilitarian, like a hotel. The man opens a door labeled Tickled Pink. Dez sees no lock, and he does not offer her a key.

"This is your room, Miss Lane," he says with no inflection at all. "Should you need anything day or night, please ring the bell, and we will be happy to attend you."

"Am I not staying in Patrick's suite?"

A small frown of disapproval. "Family suites are for family, Miss Lane."

"Do I get a key?"

He holds up the paperwork as if to remind her that she has promised not to inconvenience the staff. "Our guest rooms do not require locks, Miss Lane." With a curt bow of his head, he disappears, leaving the door open.

The room is tastefully decorated in shades of ballerina pink, burgundy, and the tender green of spring leaves. A large window looks out at the shifting blue waters, framing the garden she passed through on the way in. She'd hoped to be able to see the horses from here, but she'll settle for immaculate grounds, a sparkling oasis, and moody waves. Her suitcase isn't visible, and she wonders if perhaps it was put in Patrick's room instead, but when she opens the armoire, she finds her dresses already hung up on wooden hangers and her shoes neatly arranged along the bottom shelf. Her more personal items fill the drawers, and she's scandalized and more than a little enraged to see that someone has prominently set out her birth control pills and a few of her more adult belongings, which she packed discreetly because she knew full well that Patrick would expect generous thanks for bringing her along.

This is a message, she thinks.

They really do know everything.

She glances around the room, wondering if there are any cameras hidden anywhere. If so, they're not obvious, but nothing here would be. Tasteful and obvious are opposites. She has to assume they'll be watching somehow, whoever *they* are.

She didn't bring a laptop or tablet, but her phone should still be in her purse. According to the documents she just signed, even having it in her room right now could land her in enormous legal and financial trouble. And yet — where is her purse? She had it in the car and on the boat, but at some point, it left her possession. Did the man in pink take it? Did Patrick slip it off her shoulder, and she simply didn't notice because she was so overwhelmed by the backdrop of unrestrained opulence?

Ah. Her purse is sitting neatly on the bed, leaning against the wall of pillows. A sudden desperate sense of possession overwhelms her, and she hurries across the room to reclaim it. But when she unhooks the wicker closure, her phone is decidedly absent, as is her wallet. Nothing else seems to be missing, but the feeling is deeply unsettling.

She has no phone. No social media. No texting. No internet. No driver's license. No credit cards. No way to contact the world outside the island — or Island, as it was listed in the paperwork. As she looks around the well-appointed room, even nicer than the rooms her mother cleans at the Cosmopolitan, she doesn't see a landline, either. Only a brass button on the wall by the light switch, labeled *Please press for immediate service*. The sign strikes her as... prissy. Maybe it's the font or the little roses in the corners. The bell does not want to be pressed. They will not welcome her interruption. The *please* feels like a threat.

There's something very sinister about taking away someone's freedom like this, and yet... well, look at this place. Patrick's family comes from insane generational wealth. They built this home a hundred years ago, and they've only grown in power and prosperity since then. If they didn't have a knack for protecting every aspect of their lives, they would've lost it or sold it long ago, and this would be just another Hilton hotel filled with gracefully aging women in wide hats and muumuus and men in expensive diver watches who never seem satisfied with anything.

Everyone in the world has heard of the Ruskins. This island retreat is the one place where they can be themselves, far from the paparazzi, the phone cameras in restaurants, the numerous people that use deception to get near them.

And, yes, Dez is one of them.

Not because she wants to steal secrets or cufflinks, but because she wants to learn from Marie Caulfield-Ruskin. She just wants a foot in the door, just wants the same chance as someone born with enough money to matter, just wants the opportunity to show off her skills and intelligence instead of being instantly rejected by a hiring system designed to kick out anyone who doesn't have the ten years of experience an entry-level job now requires. She wants to *work*.

And that's why, instead of focusing on the fact that she's been separated from all of her resources, she pulls out her bikini and coverup and heads to the bathroom to make sure not a single hair is out of place. It feels strange, leaving the door unlocked while she changes clothes, but what choice does she have? If they want to come in, they will. And it's not like theft should be a problem here. They've already taken everything valuable in her luggage, and she's fairly certain Patrick's bag costs as much as her entire wardrobe, excluding the Prada dress he recently gifted her. The thing about growing up poor is that she always feels as if she's on the verge of destitution, as if everything she has can be stolen at any moment. She must keep reminding herself that this is a family home, not a hotel, even if it feels very much like a hotel.

Clad in a wide sunhat, sunglasses, bikini, lace coverup, and sandals, her tote under her arm and her sunblock already carefully applied, Dez retraces her steps back out to the pool.

Ah, but they want her to get to know the wives, which means they have hopes that she might stick around. She needs any allies she can find here, and she's good with little kids, so instead of angling toward the absolute pleasure of a flat, silent pool, she follows the white shell path around the side of the house, expecting that she'll find the other pool eventually.

"Can I help you, Miss Lane?" It's the man in pink — or another man in pink. She still doesn't know if she's seeing the same one over and over or different ones.

"I'm looking for the other pool?"

"This way."

He continues along the same path she was already taking, and she follows, slightly annoyed that he can't just point her in the right direction. She's not an idiot, and the Island is clearly a finite place of well-defined routes. There is a tricky bit of hedge maze around the corner of the house, and then she can hear the noise of children screeching and splashing. The pool comes into view, and while the other one was obviously built to be beautiful and impress, this one makes a few concessions toward actual fun. There's a bright blue water slide, two diving boards, and a zero-entry beach, as well as several lounge chairs and tables under umbrellas.

Dez pauses before she's noticed, taking stock. There are two women in their twenties on the lounge chairs, as far away from each other as they can possibly be while remaining in the area, while two female servants in sensible one-piece pink suits and matching swim caps tend to the children. Three boys, who all look like miniature versions of Patrick and his father, are running wild, splashing and jumping. The youngest is perhaps five, the oldest closer to ten. The middle one is merely a screeching blur.

"Who's that?" asks the youngest child, and the pool goes silent as everyone stares at Dez.

She has no choice but to step fully out of the shade, wearing her brightest smile. "I'm Dez. I came with Patrick. Bill said I might find y'all out here."

The two women are on alert now, examining her over their sunglasses with utmost suspicion. They share a look and rise, approaching from opposite sides before meeting Dez at the corner.

"Will said Patrick was bringing a girl," one says, a tall and willowy model type with perfect balayage and a bikini as white and small as her teeth.

"You're the first one he's brought, actually," the other one adds. She's also achingly gorgeous but a little shorter and hugely pregnant, wearing a coverup splashed with peacocks over her bump. Her hair has that orangey, fried look of someone with dark hair desperately chasing blond.

The children are still gaping at Dez, and one of the nannies says, "Come on, boys, who can make the biggest splash?"

That breaks the spell, and the women head to a table with an umbrella, bringing Dez along with them.

"I'm Genevieve," says the tall one, "Will's wife. And this is Christiane, Anthony's wife. Do you have a ring yet?"

Dez looks down at her obviously ringless finger. "No, but it's still new. This place is so beautiful. Do you get to come here often?"

Genevieve and Christiane exchange a wary look.

"Easter, always. Thanksgiving and Christmas. Fourth of July sometimes. It depends what everyone is up to," Christiane says. "How are you settling in?"

Dez takes a deep breath, uncertain how honest to be. "I'm not used to people going through my things, so that was a bit of a surprise."

Christiane sits forward, one hand on her belly. "Patrick didn't warn you? Like, at all?"

A small shrug. "Not really. I guess when you're accustomed to something, you don't really think about it." She watches their children tirelessly jumping in the pool, paddling to the side, and jumping again. The nannies must be exhausted. Dez is slightly surprised that they're so young — if she had a handsome, wealthy husband, she would only want to hire motherly, caring women who look like Winston Churchill. "These Ruskin men throw hard, huh? Your boys are all so beautiful."

Christiane's manicured hand rubs her belly possessively. "Little carbon copies," she says with something approaching sadness.

"Do you know if this one is a girl or a boy?"

Christiane looks down, wry. "It's a boy. They're always boys. Ruskins only have boys."

Dez knows this is impossible, but she's not about to argue, especially when the current sample size of four brothers and four sons suggests the impossible is correct.

"So did they take anything?" Genevieve asks impishly.

"Who?"

"When they went through your bags."

Dez is taken aback by the question. "Oh, you know. Only the basics I need to survive. My phone, my wallet, that sort of thing."

"Did you bring anything pink?"

Dez scrolls through her packing list in her head. "Just a vintage sundress. It's not my best color."

"Did they take it?"

"I... didn't check."

Genevieve laughs lightly, like this is some sort of game. "It'll be gone when you get back to your room. No one but the staff is allowed to wear pink here. My whole wardrobe was pink, the first time I came. I had my colors done and it's my best shade. But Marie refilled my wardrobe, so it wasn't much of a loss. Pretty handy, having a mother-in-law with a bottomless closet. Right?"

They both stare at Dez with the intensity of a bird watching a worm, but she refuses to squirm. "I wouldn't know, but that's really nice of her, to take care of you like that."

A wild, strangled laugh escapes Genevieve's surgically enhanced lips. "Yeah. Nice. Marie is *nice*. That's a good one. Aaaaanyway, if you want any peace, you should probably hit the other pool. They're not going to stop screaming."

Christiane reaches into her tote and holds out a wrapped set of neon orange earplugs. "Please. Take them. It's the only way you're going to survive."

Dez accepts the earplugs, and the boys must notice, because they all start straight-up screaming bloody murder. The nannies try to quiet them and fail.

"You get used to it," Christiane says as if tired to her bones, and Dez notices the purple splotches under her eyes, shining through the layers of makeup and defying the thick concealer.

"So what do you do for fun here?" Dez asks, changing the subject.

But the women just give one another that same knowing look as they stand and head back to their chairs at opposite ends of the pool. Dez is left alone at the table, holding the earplugs as three young boys stare at her, screaming again and again, their faces filled with malicious glee.

6

The other pool is pleasantly silent, the mass of the house and the hedges conspiring with the sea wind to whisk away the playful and yet aggressively goading screams of the children. Dez selects a lounger and pulls out her book. Once she's so hot she can't stand it, she sheds her coverup, checks her bikini ties, and dives into the pool. She swims back and forth a few times, only slightly embarrassed by her sloppy strokes, developed on special occasions in the hotel pool with her mom. She's not a terribly competent swimmer and has never had a pool to herself before, so she holds her nose and dives down to the bottom of the deep end and stares up at the bright blue sky, pretending that she's Ariel looking up from her secret grotto of forks and candelabras.

A man in pink is suddenly standing at the edge of the pool, staring down at her.

She gasps just the tiniest bit, and water fills her lungs. She pushes hard up to the surface and coughs as she dog-paddles to the opposite side of the pool from where the man stands, staring at her as she struggles. There's something cold in his eyes that she does not like.

"Mr. Ruskin has suggested you prepare for dinner," he says, with no apology for surprising her — and nearly drowning her.

"What time is it?"

"Five. Dinner will be served at six."

He turns on his heel and leaves, and she clings to the side of the pool, feeling as if her lungs are coated in rust. What is the point of being rich, she thinks, if your staff is constantly making you uncomfortable?

Or maybe it's just her. They likely don't treat Marie and Bill this way. And she's already seen Patrick berate a server for some small perceived slight. But shouldn't they be kind to guests? It's baffling, how ungraciously she's been treated since setting foot on the Island — by both the Ruskins and their staff. Even the wives seemed to view her as a peculiarity, not a potential friend. The children saw her as someone new to torment. While it's true that she has no genuine feelings for Patrick, she's fully committed to pretending that she does, and she's sensitive to the fact that her welcome has not been a warm one.

Dez glances around but doesn't see anyone else in the area. She pulls herself up on the side of the pool — no ladders here, oddly, probably not part of the aesthetic — and shivers as the sea wind strikes her. Someone has left a fluffy pink towel on her lounge chair, and she wraps herself up in the scent of roses and something else, something herbal. She wonders why Patrick didn't come talk to her himself; if, like the moms at the pool, he farms out his duties while he's here. She knows she has one duty of her own that cannot be farmed out, and although she doesn't have any hang-ups about sex and long ago decided to rock his world, she's not really looking forward to fucking in his suite, surrounded, she's assuming, by yet more pink walls and bound by a door with no lock. She imagines he is the kind of man who will pump away like a dog humping a rubber plant with veins pulsing in his forehead and then roll over and disinterestedly ask her if she came.

Upstairs, she finds a brand-new dress laid out on her bed, a black and white Chanel in exactly her size and tailored to her height. Not perfectly her taste, but expensive as hell and gorgeous, the kind of dress she's dreamed of touching — and eventually designing. Dez is very proud of her wardrobe and would be offended that it wasn't considered good enough... if this wasn't a Chanel. She contemplates wearing one of her own designs instead but decides that's a little too forward for her first meeting with Marie. She can't appear too eager. Eagerness, to the upper classes, can appear so tawdry — she learned that cleaning rooms with her mother.

She rids herself of the scent of chlorine in the well-appointed shower, unsurprised that all the bath products smell of roses. Thank goodness her own shampoo and conditioner haven't been confiscated; her curly hair is a very particular sort of beast. With all the work it takes to get ready, she has to hurry toward the end, determined not to arrive late.

When she steps out of the bathroom to select her shoes, she finds Patrick sitting on her bed in a sharp navy suit and perfectly tied tie. His brow immediately rumples down.

"Not my favorite dress," he admits.

"I assume your mother chose it. I found it laid out on the bed."

A chuckle. "Yeah, definitely her taste. You have to wear it then. Shall we?"

Dez slips on her black pumps and takes his arm. "So how was tennis?"

"Tennis?"

An awkward pause.

"Your dad said you guys were playing tennis with your grandfather, I thought."

He catches up. "Yeah. Tennis. Great. I'm a little stiff. Always am, the first day. Did you meet the wives?"

Dez notices he doesn't use their actual names. "Yeah. But I went back to the other pool. It was quieter."

"The boys are wild."

"They were... very spirited. I was surprised. Nobody even tried to settle them down. There was a lot of screaming."

He looks at her like she's an adorable idiot. "You can't tell a Ruskin boy what to do. That's just not how it works here."

Dez immediately hates this; children need to be told no. It's been clear over the last few weeks that Patrick does not do well with boundaries, and she's beginning to see why. With a normal suitor, she would start a lively argument, feel him out as a real future prospect, shut him down and leave once his true colors came out. But she's only using Patrick to get to his mom, so she doesn't feel that same bone-deep need to be seen and heard, to express herself, to establish herself, to fight back.

They're only here for two more days. She only has to put up with this bizarre place and Patrick's bland entitlement for two more days.

Well, if she can convince Marie to give her a chance, she might have to put on her brightest smile and keep up the charade a while longer. She can do that. She can pretend. It's what her mother does every day, after all, and stroking Patrick's ego is a lot less work than cleaning twenty trashed hotel rooms. All she wants is enough time at *Nouveau* to leverage a job offer at a fashion house. She just needs a single line on her resume.

As Patrick leads her down the grand staircase and through a different hall, Dez expects to hear the normal sounds of a big, busy family meeting to celebrate. At the very least, the boys should be running around and acting boisterous, family members calling out greetings and giving side hugs and cheek kisses. And yet the hallway is oddly silent but for the clink of glasses.

They pause in the wide, arched doorway, and even though Dez knows this place is next level, she is struck by the lavishness of the scene. The dining table is twenty feet long, solid wood and gleaming. It must've been built in the room because it looks too heavy to move without a bulldozer. The chairs are high-backed, the chandelier sprawling. The walls are high and pink, the ceiling painted with a coterie of chubby cherubs fluttering around sunrise-splashed clouds.

At the head of the table stands a man in his eighties, his face firmly set in a scowl. His tailored navy suit, just like Patrick's, highlights the width of his shoulders and the trimness of his waist. He looks spry, like he's been formed of twisted steel wire, and now Dez doesn't doubt his tennis prowess. She wonders, in fact, if he's a vampire or has been drinking at some fountain of youth, because this man looks sharp as a steel trap and just as tough.

Seated in a wheelchair at the foot of a table and wearing a Chanel dress almost identical to the one supplied for Dez is an elderly woman crafted of the same stern stuff. Her sleek white hair is pulled back in a chignon, and her skin is deeply tanned and artificially smooth, her makeup flawless. The magenta shade of her lipstick is familiar somehow, and Dez wonders if her mouth even knows how to smile. To the right of the old man is Bill Ruskin, now dressed for dinner in that same navy suit and tie, and Dez's heart splutters when she finally realizes she's breathing the same air as Marie Caulfield-Ruskin, who is also wearing a Chanel, along with her trademark platinum bob and a long string of pearls that once belonged to Marie Antoinette, which Bill bought for eight million dollars twenty years ago as an anniversary gift. Dez read an article about how they came from a hairpiece Marie wore in a famous painting, and that this Marie is never photographed without them.

There are far more men than women at the table, all with that very particular Ruskin look — sandy hair, blue-gray hazel eyes, thick brows, an athletic build, although one of the old men has a paunch. Patrick leads Dez to the final pair of chairs and holds hers out so she can sit. His manners, at least, are impeccable; at some point, Ruskin boys must become teachable.

Once Patrick has taken his seat, the old man remains standing. He looks at each of them in turn, and when his clear gray eyes alight on Dez, as piercing as an eagle, she feels as if she is staring directly into a storm.

"Welcome, family and guests," he says, his voice firm and commanding. "It is always a joy to see you gathered here, at the home built by our progenitor so long ago. I remember fondly my boyhood days on this very island, although it was a good bit wilder then." He cracks a smile, and Dez can see how this man commands a board room. "Only one pool and no slide."

Everyone chuckles, but it's forced, like the laugh track of a bad sitcom.

It is then that Dez notices the children are absent. She might actually be the youngest person here. How strange, that a family get-together would exclude the children, especially when dinner is held so early. Perhaps they're too rambunctious for the old man's taste.

"May we all enjoy this time together, that we might go out into the world again refreshed and continue our path to triumph," he says.

Everyone at the table raises a glass of rosé that Dez hadn't noticed. She swiftly picks up her glass and holds it aloft.

"To the Ruskin supremacy!"

"To the Ruskin supremacy!"

The words feel hollow and sick in Dez's mouth. Supremacy is no longer a word that carries any innocence, and if the old man doesn't know that, someone should probably tell him.

A line of servants appears with silver platters of delicate hors d'oeuvres. They are all female, in their late teens and early twenties, dressed identically in matching pink kerchiefs with calf-length pink dresses and white pocket aprons like something a fifties housewife might wear, demure and yet with an undercurrent of sexuality. Even their Keds are pink, worn with those silvery tan stockings that ice skaters wear. Many are beautiful, some are average looking, but none are hideous, and all are wearing the sort of tastefully done makeup that modern men believe to be natural when it actually takes half an hour.

One of the women places a dish of caviar-topped blinis beside Dez's plate, and she realizes what's bugging her —

Everyone on this island is white.

All the Ruskin family members and every servant she's seen is white.

And the way the old man said 'supremacy'...

A moue of distaste shivers up Dez's spine.

She nibbles at her blini, hating it, smiling like she loves it, and considers whether it's more racist to actively select other races to serve you hand and foot or to not offer them the same opportunity to thrive. If Patrick were a more intelligent, thoughtful man, she would ask him, but she instinctually knows that such a question would not bode well for any sort of future in which Marie does her a favor. The kind of people who make such choices don't wish to discuss them, which is why they live on private islands in the first place.

Course after course is served by the same eight women in their same pink dresses. Mr. Rose stands stiffly in the door to the kitchen, making sure everything runs perfectly. Plates disappear and are replaced, and the army of utensils lined up on either side of Dez's plate loses its soldiers one by one. She read up on such things before coming here, but still she checks to see which fork everyone else is using before daring to touch the silver. As they eat, there is no small talk. There is no music. They are totally silent.

It is otherworldly in its strangeness.

But again, this is the first time Dez has been privy to this life. Maybe the elders prefer silence. Maybe this is some sort of tradition. Maybe they're prone to arguing, and some unspoken edict has been passed. There's definitely an undercurrent of tension. Patrick told her that his brother Luke had been disinherited; maybe that caused some sort of rift. She hasn't even been introduced to all of the people here, and she can feel the eyes of the paunchy uncle roving over her thoughtfully, measuringly. It is not a nice feeling.

After nine courses, the last plates are whisked away. Dez ate lightly of everything and sipped delicately at her wine, knowing she has to stay sharp and on her best behavior. The food was excellent, but no one seemed to truly enjoy it. There was no gusto, no little bobbing dance of happiness, no requests for seconds, no compliments to the chef. No one seems particularly pleased or at ease. What's the point of all this money if you're so goddamned dull?

The old man stands, and everyone else follows, except for Grandmother, of course. Without a word, they form an orderly line and follow him down the hall to a large recreation room, where Mr. Rose takes his place behind a carved bar that looks like it was imported directly from Ireland. The men jockey for drinks as the women take up individual posts around the room like elegant, stuffy gargoyles in identical Chanel. Dez keeps her posture sharp, her smile bright. Marie is near. Perhaps it is time to approach.

But Patrick pulls her over to a couch, sits down and draws her into his lap. It's uncomfortable, thanks to the dress and the company, but she allows it.

"Did you like dinner?" he asks. "They bring in seafood fresh daily. It's caught just offshore."

"It was delicious." Her enthusiasm is a lie; it was good, but there was no soul to it. Her mom's boxed mac 'n' cheese is cooked with more love. "So who are all these people?" She wiggles a little to encourage him, and his hand slips down to secretly caress her.

"Grandfather and Grandmother are pretty obvious. William Ruskin II and Eleanor. She founded a perfume house in the sixties, invented the world's most popular lipstick, got bored and sold her company in the nineties. And, of course, Father and Mother you know."

"I haven't met your mother yet…"

He waves that away. "You will. Now *that* is Grandfather's middle brother, Frank." He points to the paunchy old uncle. "Never really did anything useful. Likes the racetrack. My father's youngest brother, James, will be here tomorrow. Neither of them ever got married. You met the wives…" He gazes longingly to the bar as if denied a place there. "And those are my brothers Will and Anthony."

"Where are the kids?"

He looks at her like this is a very strange question. "With their nannies? How the hell would I know? Grandfather hates noise, so dinner has always been adults only. I was pretty surprised, the first time I got to join — figured it would be some big, crazy party, but then it was totally silent. They made me wear a suit, and I thought the food was gross."

"Then what happened?"

"I grew up." His hand abandons her rump, and he scoots her off his lap and stands, smoothing down his pants. "Can I get you a drink?"

"Please. Whatever sounds good."

Because so far, he's been the kind of guy who prefers it when she doesn't make requests or have firm opinions. It doesn't matter. She's not a huge drinker, and she doesn't plan on getting tipsy, not with Marie just across the room, hip against the pool table, watching her with the flat black doll eyes of shark.

Patrick brings Dez a martini with two olives, and she wishes she'd given him a little more direction as she thinks it tastes like worms. Still, it's the same thing Grandmother and Marie are having, so she'll learn how to love it.

Genevieve and Christiane disappear, Grandmother rolls away in her wheelchair, and Patrick leaves Dez alone on the sofa to go chat with his brothers. She waffles on whether or not she should introduce herself to her idol. It's normal, meeting the mother of a significant other while on holiday; in fact, it's odd that Marie hasn't greeted her and Patrick hasn't presented her. Dez stands and smooths down her dress.

As if sensing her readiness, Marie places the dregs of her martini on the pool table and slips out the door. Dez waits thirty seconds and follows.

A man in pink is waiting outside and blocks her way, taking her elbow.

"Can I help you, Miss Lane?"

"The restroom?" she says, jerking her elbow a little. He does not loosen his grip.

He leads her upstairs — to one of the suites. When he opens the door, she sees something scant and lacy laid out on the four-poster king bed.

"Mr. Ruskin will join you shortly," the man says.

"How — ?" she begins.

But the man in pink is gone. There is a bruise on her elbow.

She uses the restroom, puts on the negligee, and waits in the center of the enormous bed, wondering what the fuck is wrong with these people.

7

Patrick arrives, and Dez does everything she can to please him. It's exactly the sort of sex she thought it would be, right down to the veins in his forehead, and then he rolls over and goes to sleep without asking her if she did, in fact, come. She did not.

She stands there, staring at the discarded condom on the floor, wondering if he's ever had to pick up after himself a day in his life. She leaves it there and returns to her own room to freshen up. He did not invite her to stay, didn't reach out sleepily to cuddle her, didn't even pat her ass and tell her good game. His needs have been met, and hers have not, and now she just wants a good shower.

Once she's smelling of roses and in her pajamas, Dez the night owl doesn't know what to do with herself. There's a big TV with a thousand channels, but there is no Netflix, no Hulu, no comforting Keep Watching queue with her favorite shows. She pulls out her book, but all the words run together. She realizes that she's... well, not hungry. But something. What's the Japanese word for when you eat because your mouth is lonely?

She can't look it up. They took her phone.

What's the word for when everything is lonely?

The castle, her room, the Island is lonely.

Full of energy and vaguely aware that it's not even ten, she opens her door and considers the hallway. She doesn't see anyone, but every time she tries to go anywhere, some dude in all pink shows up to redirect her. She's still mad about her elbow. She'd rather die than press the brass button.

But one thing she does know is that most places have a back stairwell for staff. No one is huffing laundry up and down that wide, grand staircase, where the paterfamilias might have to see someone else's dirty undies. She considers the doors beyond her own, each marked with what she decides must be the names of roses — Sweet Wonder, Times Past, Joie de Vivre — and finds one at the end of the hallway with no sign. When she gingerly pushes it open, she finds a cramped stairwell lit with bare bulbs. Success! She scurries down the staircase, as quiet as a mouse. It feels more like home than anything else on the Island.

The stairwell continues downward and ends in two doors, one of which must lead outside. Well, of course. Because the laundry has to go somewhere out of sight. She saw the other buildings as the boat approached, so it would make sense if the staff did their business elsewhere. Dez takes the door to the main house, hoping to find the kitchen for a late-night nibble. A place like this must keep a bag of Cheetos around for the kids, right? Even the most spoiled little boys don't want caviar all the time.

Thanks to her socks, she's silent on the marble, the house preternaturally still. That's when she realizes there are no pets here — no carefully groomed dogs or giant fish tanks or peacocks or whatever rich people keep on leashes. There are horses outside, but she still hasn't seen them. She'll have to ask Patrick for a tour of the stables tomorrow. Maybe she can give one of the horses a carrot.

Finally she hears the clatter of silver and porcelain and is soon standing in the wide door to the kitchen, where four women in pink dresses bustle about, doing the mountain of dishes produced at dinner. She doesn't see a dishwasher, just four identical pink backs in an assembly line, washing, rinsing, drying, and stacking.

"It's just so much. I just... I don't know," one woman starts — the stacker.

"You *never* know. That's the problem. That's why they get away with it," snaps the one washing.

"Get away with it? Come on." The rinser snorts. "This is so far beyond 'getting away with it'. There's a world out there — "

"But is this our only choice?" asks the dryer. "There's got to be some other way. I feel sick — "

Crash.

The girl stacking plates has just dropped one, and she's looking right at Dez, her blue-gray eyes huge in her pale face.

"Miss Lane! Please. You can't be here," she says, rushing forward with the dish towel still in hand.

The other three spin around looking something between guilty and angry.

"I'll handle it," says the washer, who looks the angriest. She strips off her elbow-length pink gloves and strides forward like a tornado. "Let me escort you back to your room. Please."

"I'm so sorry to interrupt," Dez says softly, guiltily, only now realizing that this sort of thing was covered in the paperwork she signed, and that instead of making their jobs easier by secretly grabbing a bag of Cheetos, she has made their jobs harder. "I just wanted a snack…"

"You can always press the button. That's why it's there."

"I didn't want to be a bother."

The girl sighs and tucks light brown hair under her kerchief; the hot water has left her a little bedraggled, her mascara running. She looks exhausted and annoyed, but not necessarily at Dez.

"What do you want? Leftovers, or real food?"

Dez could cry, she's so happy at that offer. "I was hoping for Cheetos."

The rinser chuckles. "Yeah, not on the Island. God forbid."

"Behave!" the dryer hisses. She goes into a walk-in pantry and returns with a banana, an apple, and a big, plastic-wrapped cookie. "Will this work?"

Dez takes them. "God, yes. Thank you so much. It's not that dinner wasn't delicious — "

"We understand. Now, please let me escort you back upstairs, Miss Lane."

The washer goes to stand by the door, eyebrows up. There's something familiar about her, but Dez isn't sure what, something beyond noticing her as one of the servers at dinner.

"I came down the back stairs. Can I go that way again? I didn't want to cause any extra work, and I don't want to get anyone in trouble…"

The woman's eyes go wide with fear. "Oh, Miss Lane. It would be best for all involved if you refrained from using the staff passages. Your NDA should've mentioned it. They're sticklers for that."

She looks so panicked that Dez floods with shame. She wasn't prepared for how serious everything is here.

"I'm sorry. I was just trying to stay out of the way. I'll stick to the proper stairs in the future. I hope I haven't inconvenienced anyone." She walks to the door and follows the woman out, glancing back over her shoulder at the girls still waiting at the sink and giving them a little wave; they all seem to be about her age, give or take four years. "Thanks. Sorry. Thanks," she says, feeling that it's still somehow insufficient.

The woman is silent as she leads Dez up the grand staircase, past the row of suites, around the corner, and to her door.

"Thanks again," Dez says. "And sorry again, too."

The woman — girl? — gives her a sad smile. "No one on the Island ever says they're sorry for anything. Are you sure you're supposed to be here?"

With a different inflection, this could be an insult, but Dez takes it as a compliment. "My mom is a housekeeper for a big hotel," she admits. "I spent a lot of time helping her make beds when I was little. I'm not used to being…"

"On this side of the vacuum?" the girl supplies.

"Yeah, that. It seems like a difficult place to work."

The girl's face goes completely and professionally blank, their odd moment of shared empathy gone.

"We are here to serve, Miss Lane. Please press the button next time, should you need anything. It will be better for us all."

With a bobbed curtsey, she disappears down the staff stairwell.

Safely back in her room, Dez eats her banana and thinks about how bizarre that whole situation was. She isn't used to so many rules taken so seriously, so many strange lines waiting to be crossed.

When she wakes up, there's a pink sticky note on the pillow beside her.

On it are written three words in plain black ink.

GO HOME. NOW.

8

Dez does not tell Patrick about the note. She hides it under her mattress, uncertain what it means. Is it from someone in the family — one of the strange, cold wives or the aggressively staring grandparents? Was it one of the girls from the kitchen last night, maybe even the one who escorted her back to her room, after she bungled their conversation? Was it — certainly not Marie?

No. Marie hasn't even met her. If she wanted Dez to leave, she would simply tell her to do so, or dispatch one of the many servants to drag her away.

She hasn't been given a schedule, so she's surprised when she shows up to a breakfast that is clearly ending. Chafing dishes are being cleared away by the women in their pink uniforms while a few stragglers in crisp business casual sip coffee from tiny white porcelain cups. Marie is gone, if she was ever there, ending a fond daydream of breaking the ice over croissants. Dez is furious with herself, but also with them — and especially with

Patrick. With no phone, no alarm clock, how should she know when anything is happening? There's a little gold clock in her room, the kind that sits under a dome and constantly spins its elegant arms like a bored octopus, but it's not like she can tell it to wake her up at whatever-the-hell time.

Patrick looks up from his coffee, sees her, frowns, and hurries over. He doesn't speak until they're in the hall, around the corner, out of earshot.

"Why are you still in your pajamas? Christ, Dez, it's nine thirty. Breakfast is at eight."

"You didn't say anything. I didn't know," she says as he steers her back toward the steps.

"Well now you do. Breakfast at eight, lunch at noon, dinner at six. Just ring the bell and tell them to wake you up whenever you need. It's simple. Now go get dressed. This isn't a kid's slumber party."

Having deposited her at the stairwell, he returns to the dining room, and Dez's cheeks redden with shame as she scurries back to her room and prepares herself to face Patrick and his family again. It was silly, just wandering downstairs like this was a normal house for normal people. She'd showered, at least, so now she just has to choose the armor of her own uniform. She doesn't know what's on the docket today, so she puts on a sundress she designed and sandals she painted to match, finger-combs her hair, carefully applies a full face of makeup. At any moment, she might be called into a private corner by Marie for their official introduction, and she must look the part.

She does notice, while flipping through her wardrobe options, that Genevieve was right — her only pink dress has been removed. She wonders if it will be returned when she departs the Island, if there is some pink-painted jail somewhere for clothes that dare to defy the local dress code.

There are two hours until lunch, but when Dez returns to the dining room, it's empty of Ruskins. She'd assumed Patrick would be waiting for her, but she's assumed a lot about how Patrick will treat her here, apparently.

"Where is everyone?" she asks a — well, *maid* feels like the wrong word. *Servant* does, too.

The woman looks up with a practiced smile. "You might find them at the stables, Miss Lane. I believe there was some interest in the new foal."

Dez returns the smile. "Thanks. I'll go check. Can't go wrong with baby horses, right?"

The woman looks at her like she's demented. "I suppose not."

Heading outside, Dez prepares herself to find a man in pink swooping in like a polite vulture, but for once, she has a little freedom to roam. She has a general idea of where to find the stables, so she follows the white shell path around the side of the house she hasn't seen yet. It's immediately obvious that she's chosen the correct route, as the path widens, bordered by a shining white picket fence. Dez has no idea how such perfectly green grass can grow on an island that should be mostly sand, but the effect is charming and magical. A long, elegant pink barn runs along the other side of the fence. It seems a strange color for a barn, but it flawlessly matches the shape and architecture of all the other buildings on the Island, and a big red barn with SEE RUSKIN CITY would definitely look out of place, so she's not sure why she's surprised. Figures cluster just outside, and Dez hopes Patrick is among them. She doesn't particularly like him, but at least he's vaguely familiar. She's learning that everyone else in his family is some kind of cryptid, that the Very, Very Rich live on a plane of existence that she can't quite access.

A horse bugles, and Dez looks up to find what seems like a whole herd of monstrous beasts galloping directly at her. She knows there's a fence between them, and yet — the horses are so big, so loud, so powerful. She's never really been that close to them before, for all that she's dreamed of them since she was small.

These horses…

They don't look nice.

They're sleek and brown to a one, huge, glossy, thundering toward her, and she takes a step back from the fence, then another, then another. The horses aren't slowing down, aren't stopping, she can see the whites of their eyes, the muscles of their chests, the froth billowing from their sharp white teeth.

She's about to turn and run when the horses, almost like marionettes controlled by the same puppeteer, skid to a stop. The first one rams into the fence, but not with full force, just enough to rattle it, to rattle her. The giant head hangs over the white wood boards, the teeth clacking at her and the big nostrils flaring like the horse is scenting for blood.

"Miss Lane, please give the ponies space." A man in pink grasps her elbow to tug her away, and she rips her arm out of his grip before he can give her another bruise.

"I am," she says sharply. "I'm well on my side of the fence. Tell them to give *me* space."

It comes out breathy and rattled, this little defiance.

She hates that she sounds this frightened, this out of sorts.

At least none of the Ruskins are close enough to see her like this.

The man in pink stares at her, expressionless, as if he'd like to say more, but something is holding him back. She sees herself in the mirrored lenses of his sunglasses. Her skin is flushed, her hair wild, her eyes goggling like some strange sea creature gasping for breath on the land where it never belonged.

"You can't bother the ponies," Patrick calls as he, again, hurries toward her.

"I was literally just walking along a path. I'm not sure what I did that offended them — "

"They're not used to outsiders," the man in pink says quietly.

"Do they eat them, or…?"

Does she imagine the man in pink chuckles?

Surely not.

Patrick reaches her, and she faces him as if daring him to try to take her elbow. "I just wanted to see the foal," she says, almost begging. "I heard there was a baby horse."

He looks at her like she's a naughty but ignorant child. "There is. Come on. But sort yourself out. You look crazy. The horses won't hurt you."

Dez is looking at them as they in turn regard her.

She is fairly certain the lead horse would bite a meaty chunk out of her shoulder if given the chance. It looks mean. She does not say this. She knows which of them actually belongs on the Island.

She smooths her hair down and takes a deep breath, giving Patrick the sort of bright, admiring look he drinks up. "I hope I look okay now. Do they have names?"

The man in pink follows at a respectful distance as Patrick and Dez walk side by side toward the barn. Patrick tells her the horses all have long, intricate names based on their bloodlines but that the family always gives them rose-related nicknames. Thorn, Bloom, Blush, Roam.

"You guys are really all in on roses, huh?"

His gaze is fond but patronizing, like she should already know this. "Ruskin. Rose, kin. We can trace our ancestors back forever over in England."

Finally, that's one question firmly answered.

They reach the barn, where the grand doors are thrown open. For a big, heavy thing, it's decently lit and clean as bleached bone. Bill and Christiane stand at a stall door, looking in, with Christiane's son in Bill's arms. Dez is surprised by how quiet the little boy is; the last time she saw him, he was screaming at the top of his lungs. Perhaps the presence of his stern grandfather has something to do with that.

Bill's head jerks around; seeing that it's Patrick and Dez, he relaxes and goes back to talking. "Born just last week. Solid bloodlines, and her dam was a champion."

"We don't say 'dam', Papa. It's a bad word."

Bill laughs. "It's the proper word for a mother horse, but we only use it that way in the stable. What should we name her, kiddo? Do you want to name the new foal?"

The little boy, dressed all in white and pale blue, his hair still wet from where it's been carefully slicked down, solemnly says, "Pinkie Pie."

Dez is aware that this is a My Little Pony, but she suspects Bill Ruskin has no idea. "An excellent suggestion. Make the sign. But go with Pinkie."

A man in pink who Dez hadn't noticed says, "Yes, Mr. Ruskin," and hurries down the hall, disappearing around a corner. It's as if he materialized from nothing. Dez looks more closely at the stable and finds another man in pink waiting nearby in the shadows, his hands behind his back. Their outfits are the same color as all the other uniforms, of course, and they wear the same pink polo shirt, but with long pants and soft brown boots, an allowance for life in the stable. When she glances up, she sees a flash of pink in the hayloft; a woman. She squints, wondering if it's one of the girls from the kitchen, but the woman ducks out of sight.

One time, Dez went camping with the Girl Scout troop she was in for half a year, and they were sleeping in this musty bunkroom, and she noticed a spider. But as soon as she saw one, she saw hundreds, almost like a magic eye poster, spiders on the ceiling, on every windowsill, webs in every corner. She decided to quit Girl Scouts, after that; she knew it was expensive, all those trips, but it was mainly the concept of spiders that bothered her.

The Girl Scouts did a lot of things in places with spiders, and Dez could never relax, just knowing they were there. That's how she's beginning to feel about the servants in their pink outfits.

They're everywhere. Hidden. Waiting.

"Take a look, Desirée," Patrick's father says. He moves aside and inclines his head for her to peer into the stall.

Dez steps up, annoyed that everyone here keeps using her full name, which she's never really liked. Inside the stall is another enormous brown horse, but this one looks fat and tired and old, her eyes like liquid pools of melted chocolate. Beside her is a soft little foal, all legs and flicking tail and curious, long-lashed eyes.

"I don't know much about polo ponies..." She trails off, knowing Ruskin men like to talk but hate being questioned.

"We breed our own horses," Bill says, his tone warm for the first time. "Carefully continuing the bloodlines. Our polo ponies are all thoroughbreds, with excellent, traceable lineages. These aren't retired racehorses or rescue cases." He meets her eyes. "We don't let in bad blood. Every dam and sire is carefully chosen to maintain the very finest standards."

"Sounds like eugenics," she says softly, as if not wanting to frighten the foal. She knows very well what he's saying, and she knows she's expected to play along, but...

Well, fuck him.

She's not a retired racehorse or some random charity case, and she knows what he's implying.

She's smart, she's talented, and she's driven.

And she's not even here to — to *breed* with Patrick.

Doesn't want to marry him.

Doesn't even want to see him again, really.

She just wants ten minutes with Marie, and then she'll take her unpure womb back to Savannah with her.

But she can't tell Bill Ruskin that.

"Focused breeding programs produce the fastest, strongest, smartest horses," he continues — so smug, so sure. "It's not about philosophy. It's about science. This foal will be a champion one day. We only invest in champions." He looks down at her, smiling, cheek to cheek with the grandson who looks exactly like a tiny clone of him. "Isn't that right, kiddo?"

"I want to ride a horsey," the boy says.

Bill ruffles his hair. "You're almost big enough. Maybe one day you'll ride Pinkie."

"Pinkie *Pie*, Papa."

Bill ignores the correction and places the little boy on the ground, where his silent mother clutches his hand as if for dear life. "Do you ride, Desirée?"

There's a lascivious tone to the question that makes Dez blush. "I wasn't raised among champion horses, but I'm not scared of trying."

At that, Bill laughs, but there is no humor in it. He wants so badly to cow and humiliate her, she thinks, but he's amused by her unwillingness to make it easy.

"Take her out for a trot on one of the old ponies, if you like," he says to Patrick before meeting her eyes again. He does this on purpose, she thinks. It's unnerving, like staring at a statue. "You can't develop a proper seat this late — you'll never play polo — but maybe you can stay on one of our old mares long enough to see the world from a better vantage point."

Dez shrugs. "Or I could just ride a bike."

At that, he really does laugh.

"Touché, little girl. Touché."

He leaves the barn, and Christiane waddles in his wake hand-in-hand with her son, throwing Dez a glance she can't quite parse. Desperate and apologetic and also vaguely annoyed, like Dez has broken yet another unspoken rule. She's guessing that mere female partners don't talk back to their elders here.

Oh, well. She'll do as she pleases.

She's just a guest. They've made that perfectly clear.

"If you really do want to go for a ride, you'll need to change," Patrick says, all huffy, like he'll do it, but he'll be conspicuously miserable the whole time.

"I wouldn't want to slow you down."

"Oh, I'd just have one of the grooms take you. I'm kind of a 'ride fast or don't ride at all' guy." He shrugs like this sort of response doesn't make him a douchebag. "Anyway, you probably shouldn't get covered in horsehair before dinner. It's going to be a big thing, now that Uncle James is finally here. Have you seen enough of the foal? She's pretty cute, right?"

The little foal wanders near, her tiny, velvety nose snuffling. Dez holds out her hand, curious whether the baby feels as soft as she looks.

Quick as a snake, the mother horse snaps at her, teeth clacking together so close Dez feels the spray of hot horse saliva on her hand. The only reason she still has a hand is because one of the men in pink has yanked her out of the way. She doesn't know where he came from or why Patrick didn't step in instead, but she's shaking.

"Thank you," she says.

Patrick slaps the man's hand away. "Don't talk to the help, Dez."

He puts his arm around her shoulders and guides her back out into the sun.

Why does it seem like everything here has such sharp teeth?

9

Dez doesn't want to leave her room; she's still shaken from the horse incident. She'd always thought horses were sweet creatures with kind eyes, that a horse would look at her and, like a unicorn identifying a virgin, sense her inner goodness and adoration. But the horses here are like an altogether different sort of mythological monster, made of muscle and sinew and teeth and hate. She feels terribly vulnerable, her heart wounded by the fact that something actually tried to hurt her. She just wanted to pet the baby.

After considering it for a long time, she presses the button on the wall. Mere seconds pass before there's a knock on the door.

"Come in," she calls.

It's one of the men in pink, and he stands in her doorway with his hands behind his back.

"How can I help you, Miss Lane?"

"Would it be possible to take a meal here, in my room? I missed breakfast, and one of the horses tried to bite me, and…"

She's not sure how much to say, but it just tumbles out of her. "I don't think I can face the rest of them, just now. Can you — can you tell Patrick, too? That I'm going to miss lunch, but I'll definitely be there for dinner. I know it's a big deal."

"Of course, Miss Lane. What would you like?"

She looks around as if she's in a hotel. "Is there a menu? Some leftovers? I don't want to be any trouble. I'm really very easy. No allergies or anything. A PB&J would be fine."

His lips almost twitch in a smile. "The chefs would be happy to accommodate anything you wish."

That's… a lot of pressure. "Just a sandwich. Whatever is easy to make and easy for you to clean up."

"Of course, Miss Lane."

When he returns in twenty minutes, he's brought a huge tray of at least a dozen sandwiches, dainty cucumber tea sandwiches and pimento cheese sandwiches with no crusts and big, hearty Dagwood subs held together with skewers and even one pathetic, spongey thing with a little toothpick labeling it gluten free and keto. The tray also includes a salad, a bowl of freshly cut fruit, an array of condiments, and a dish of homemade potato chips, plus a bottle of water, a glass of tea, and a glass of wine.

"Oh, wow, that's a lot of food." Dez stands and approaches him, holding out a five-dollar bill she found loose in the bottom of her ransacked purse. "Is it okay to tip you? Is that allowed?"

He puts the tray on her desk and steps back, holding his hands behind his back. "We can't accept tips, but that is very kind of you. Is there anything else, Miss Lane?"

She feels silly now, like this is all too much, and she just wants to pay someone and feel like everything is equitable. The bill feels small and greasy in her hand. "No. I mean, do I just set it outside when I'm done, like in a hotel? I keep forgetting it's not a hotel."

"As you prefer, Miss Lane."

With that, he's gone, and Dez sorts through the tray's offerings. She has never felt so wasteful in her life. This is an entire week's worth of food for her, and she's fairly certain it's all just going to go down a garbage chute when she sends ninety percent of it back.

After eating, she takes a long bath in the enormous soaking tub using the supplied bath salts. The water is tinted pink, the air redolent of roses, and she wonders if being around these insufferable snobs is worth constant access to a tub in which both her tits and her knees are simultaneously underwater. She hasn't had a bath in years, nothing but dorm showers. It's the happiest she's been since she got here, the only real joy she's known, surrounded by the utmost luxury. She sips the tepid pink wine and sinks down, her tension unspooling. This, she could get used to.

At least she's ready for dinner on time. While she was in the bath, someone snuck in and left another dress on her bed, a gorgeous Versace. She's immediately admiring the fabric and seams and wonders if she gets to keep these dresses or if they're loaners. She hung the Chanel up in her closet last night, and it's still there, which gives her hope... but her next emotion is annoyance. Is her wardrobe not good enough?

In her daydreams, Marie approaches her to compliment one of the dresses she's thrifted and restyled, and it's the perfect opener to make her ambitions known. But instead, she keeps receiving these couture dresses that aren't quite her style but are stunning and valuable and...

Not her. Not her at all.

The label, yes; the matronly, conservative cut, no.

The Ruskins are turning her... into whatever they are.

She never agreed to that.

Goddammit, nothing here is going the way she'd hoped.

She still hasn't met Marie.

Doesn't that seem rude, to spend a full day in a home with your son's current girlfriend and not even bother to introduce yourself? For people so hung up on formality, this seems desperately gauche. Instead of feeling welcome, she feels more like an outsider than she'd ever dreamed possible. Even if she's slunk in amongst them like some upstart cuckoo, that doesn't mean she has no feelings. She hates them, but she wants them to love her. It's complicated.

Still, the dress fits like a glove, and she matches her makeup and jewelry to it, glad she brought her black Jimmy Choos that go with literally everything.

Patrick opens her door just before six, doesn't even bother knocking. He looks her up and down and smiles his approval. "Where'd you get that little number?"

"Someone left it on my bed."

"Someone must have good taste."

In a real relationship, she would thank him, but she knows damn well it wasn't him. None of it is him. He hasn't earned anything. He's as useless as his screaming nephews, just a little boy who thinks he rules the world.

She gives him an adoring smile. She's not giving up on her ambitions just because it's not easy. "*Someone* must."

He's in a tux, she notes — this dinner must indeed be special.

How a dinner can be more special than a nine-course meal with wine pairings on a private island she isn't certain, but she's never been to a party where people wear tuxes before, unless high school prom counts.

Patrick holds out his arm, and she takes it, and they walk down the grand stairs, and everything that should feel like a dream feels like a bad play with terrible actors. They go to a different dining room one step down from a ballroom, the table even longer and the chandelier even more grand. Huge windows open out onto balconies that look upon the sea, their filmy white curtains billowing in and out of the room. The walls are that same trademark pink, the ceiling stamped tin, bright as a mirror. Patrick leads her to their seats, which are placed similarly to last night's arrangement.

At least they're not the last ones in tonight — Will and Genevieve arrive next, then Anthony and Christiane. The men wear tuxes, the women couture gowns, both flashier than hers. Dez only knows the men from her online searches. She still hasn't actually met them. Marie Caulfield-Ruskin is just across the table, but it's too wide to accommodate conversation, and there are flower arrangements in the way, towers of small white roses, white poppies with black centers, white lilies dusted with pollen. Here and there, a gigantic, blowsy pink rose nestles like a queen, the biggest and most beautiful specimens.

A little too on the nose, but no one asked Dez.

No one speaks to Dez unless they have to.

Finally, there is only one seat left, and the old man at the head of the table smacks his hand on the wood and says, "Fetch James. Now!"

Mr. Rose hurries away from his post at the door. After a few moments of tense silence, an energetic man in his fifties trots in. He looks like a movie star —

Oh. Wait. He *is* a movie star. He goes by another last name, out in the world, but Dez would know him anywhere. He smiles his trademark smile as he sits.

"You could've started without me."

"You make a mockery of tradition!" Grandfather spits.

"It's not my tradition. I'm a second son, remember?"

Grandfather stands, his chair squealing back.

"Now that we're finally all here," he begins, voice echoing in the marble chamber as the ocean pounds outside, "we come together to celebrate Black Saturday."

Dez looks at Patrick; this is pretty weird. She knows yesterday was Good Friday, and she's heard today called Easter Eve, but Black Saturday sounds… dark.

"On this day, Christ lay enclosed in his tomb, caught between life and death." The old man pauses; the room is so quiet Dez could hear a petal drop from one of the many vases of velvety roses. "But that's not what we celebrate. On this day in 1834, our ancestor landed on this island and claimed it as his own. We were always Ruskins, but that was the day our conquest began." He holds up a hand, and a fleet of pink-clad women hurry in with trays laden with pink champagne. A flute is placed in front of every seat. Dez starts to reach for hers, but Patrick steps on her foot under the table, and she puts her hands in her lap, fuming that he would mar her most treasured pair of heels.

The old man picks up his glass, briefly making a face that suggests he's found fault with it. As if on cue, everyone else reaches for their champagne. Dez holds her glass aloft alongside everyone else, imagining what a dreary life it would be, if she had to look forward to this bizarre speech every year, to sitting here dressed to the nines for the same old people when no one seems to like each other. Or anything.

"To the Ruskins!" the old man shouts.

"To the — "

At the same moment, every window slams shut, along with every door, silencing the cheer. Servants in pink line every wall, more of them than Dez had even imagined, far more than are required to serve this meal.

"Not all the Ruskins," says one of the pink-clad women, stepping forward with a gun in her hand.

10

"What is the meaning of this?" the old man shouts. "Guns are forbidden on the Island!"

The woman — the one from the kitchen, Dez thinks, the one that took her back upstairs — steps forward, the gun pointed at the old man's heart. "What are you going to do about it, Grandfather?"

He reaches to his side, draws his own pistol — so much for forbidden — points it at her...

Click, click, click.

Nothing.

"Guns are forbidden indeed," she muses.

"Mr. Rose, stop her!"

At the old man's strangled screech, the butler darts forward from his post at the door, and Dez can see now that he's not just a butler, he's a bodyguard. His coat is cut carefully to hide his broad shoulders, but he moves like the hero of a spy movie, fast and confident. As he runs, he reaches into his coat, probably going for his own gun —

But the woman doesn't budge.

She shoots him in the knee at nearly point-blank range.

Dez has never been around guns before. The sound is blunt, startling, explosively loud, echoing around the marble room like a — like a fucking bullet.

Mr. Rose stumbles as his foot lands, the knee destroyed. He sprawls face-first on the white marble at the woman's feet, leaving a red streak behind. His gun skitters across the room, and a woman in pink hurries over to grab it, holding it like she's never seen someone hold a gun before. Another woman scurries to where Mr. Rose is moaning on the floor and slips another, smaller gun from an ankle holster, and he can't stop her because his leg doesn't work anymore.

The room is silent, but Dez sees the men at the table exchanging glances, each one using his eyes and chin to suggest the other ones do something useful. Dez looks down at the table, but there are no knives, no forks, no silverware. No plates even, just flowers and champagne flutes, which she just now notices are actually plastic instead of the expected glass. As are the vases, actually.

Not one breakable thing, not one sharp thing.

She realizes…

They planned this, the servants.

They planned this moment.

The woman with the gun takes a step back and points it at Mr. Rose, who is struggling and failing to stand.

"Go to Grandfather," she says.

"You don't tell me what to do," he hisses between broken breaths.

"The first rule of the Island is that the person with the most power makes the rules. I'm the one with the gun, so I make the rules. And I say go to Grandfather. You can crawl if you like. We'll wait."

He stares at her, hate filling his eyes, and she aims the gun at the center of his forehead.

"Ask yourself… what does she have to lose?" she says softly. "What do any of us have to lose?"

Gritting his teeth, growling, Mr. Rose crawls toward the old man, who is still standing stupidly at the head of the table, pointing his emptied gun at the woman in pink as if still hopeful it's not just a useless bit of metal. At the other end of the table, his wife looks like a statue in her wheelchair. She doesn't seem scared, or surprised. Dez wonders if she's a sociopath or has dementia or is drugged out of her mind. With rich people, it can be so hard to tell.

"Valerie, put the gun down," Bill Ruskin says from his seat, his voice firm but gentle, like he's talking to a horse.

"Or what?"

He has no answer to that.

The calculus in the room is clear. There are more people in pink than people not in pink. And now that Dez looks closely, she sees knives in the hands of some servants, a ball-peen hammer, an ice pick. Smaller things, easily concealed. Clever.

Mr. Rose leaves a slug trail of blood behind him on the marble, smeared by his shoes, and as he nears his goal, Valerie says, "Grandfather, sit back and put your feet up on the table."

"That table is Madagascar Rosewood," Grandmother observes calmly, as if unaware of the tension in the room. She has the sultry, smoky voice of a screen siren. "Brought here in 1928 at some cost. Hand carved. Rarest wood in the world."

"And Grandfather is going to put his dirty, dirty shoes on it," Valerie agrees.

Grandfather's veiny hands are in fists. "What if I don't?"

Valerie's smile is chilling. "Then things will happen faster, won't they? For the first time in your life, just do as you're told. Have a little taste of what the rest of us have to deal with all the time."

Practically vibrating with anger, the old man sits and scoots his chair back and grunts as he maneuvers his feet onto the table one by one, which is apparently no easy task at his age. He takes it slow, has to use his hands. Dez chokes down a mad sort of laugh.

This is absurd.

Completely absurd.

One of the ten richest men in the world is furiously contorted in his chair with his shiny black shoes on the table, surrounded by champagne and roses, and this — this has to be some sort of theater.

It can't be real.

"There, girl. I did as you asked. Can we stop this farce?"

"It's no farce. It's revenge. The Ruskins are the farce. This grand old family that can trace back its lineage for generations, that only makes the most advantageous matches — that's the farce."

"And what's Mr. Rose got to do with it, then?" he says tiredly, like this is not a new argument. "He's just hired help."

Valerie doesn't answer him. "Kneel by Grandfather's chair, Mr. Rose."

Mr. Rose drags himself up from the ground, grunting and groaning in extreme pain, pulling his body upward, fighting gravity and unconsciousness and blood loss. James scoots his chair away as if worried that helplessness is catching. For all that he's played policemen and army chiefs and even the president once in movies, he currently has the shifty-eyed look of a coward.

Now there is a very old man with his feet on the table, his spine curled with age and his ankles sharp and knobby in their black socks, while his much younger, stronger butler-slash-bodyguard kneels at his side, his face gray and his eyes wet with pain.

"Lick his shoes," Valerie says.

Around the outside of the room, the servants snicker like a pack of hyenas waiting for the kill.

Well, some of them.

Others look uncomfortable, like they want to run away.

And yet they don't.

"You want me to lick his shoes?" Mr. Rose asks, a ragged breath between each word.

"You're a bootlicker. An enforcer to a petty tyrant. He makes the rules, and you ensure they're followed. He says jump, you say how high. He says punish, you choose the punishment. You're the only one of us who has a choice, and yet here you are — for what, twenty years now? So go on. Lick his boots, like you always do."

The old man is wearing hard black leather shoes, the sort that only really go with tuxedos, that are expensive and painful and mostly useless. He looks over at his butler and says, peevishly, "Well, get it over with."

Mr. Rose extends his tongue and leans in, touching it to the old man's heel.

"Really get in there," Valerie says. "I know you know how."

With a look of utmost hate, Mr. Rose clears his throat and tries again, running his tongue over the side of the shoe with a rebellious sort of disdain.

There is a moment of tense silence as he licks his lips, his eyes nervously shooting back and forth as he realizes… something is very wrong.

"Tastes funny, doesn't it? Remember when you told me to make sure Grandfather's shoes were so shiny you could see your face in them for tonight's banquet? I did. But then I mixed up a little something else."

"What?"

His voice is a ragged whisper, his eyes going round and buggy. He doubles over onto his hands and knees, grimacing, and vomits blood and froth all over the marble floor. Grandfather puts a fist to his closed mouth and turns away.

"Hm. Let's see. Arsenic. Foxglove. Oleander. Hemlock." She smiles. "All things we have around the gardens or use in our flower arrangements. And a little shrimp, just to make sure. That's probably what you're tasting. That silly old allergy."

Mr. Rose pants, his face purple and bulging, his eyes streaming tears. "You… bitch…" he wheezes.

"You've called me enough names. All of us. All our lives. You all have. Ruling with an iron fist. But no more. We, your so-called servants, will take what's owed us. Tonight."

She puts a hand on the old man's shoulder as he stares down at his dying butler.

"Your time is over, Grandfather."

He looks up, eyes red and wet and raging. "I very much doubt that. This family — "

"Oh, no!" Valerie interrupts, feigning fawning concern as she runs a finger over his withered cheek. "I missed a spot when I shaved you earlier. How embarrassing. I know how much you like a close shave. I'm surprised you didn't notice. The last time I missed a spot, you gave me a black eye."

The old man looks perplexed but crafty, like there's some way he can talk her out of her nonsense. Like she's a little girl misbehaving. Valerie moves to stand behind him. One hand is on his shoulder, and the other, the hand that held the gun, disappears briefly. When it appears again, lying gently against the velvet black of his crisp tux jacket, there's something shiny there.

An old-fashioned straight razor.

Valerie leans in, her face beside his. "Grandfather, you know how you always tell us girls to smile and appreciate all that we have? Smile, or you'll give us something to frown about?"

"What — "

"Smile for me, Grandfather."

She draws the razor across his throat, and it blooms red and wet, blood pouring onto the fine grain of Madagascar Rosewood.

11

No one shouts, "Dad!" or, "Grandpa!" and rushes lovingly to Grandfather's side. No one moves. No one says anything. His own wife just stares at him like he's an incorrect dinner order at a restaurant that has landed at her table by mistake, a filet that's embarrassingly bloody.

Grandfather's mouth opens and closes, his blue eyes blinking rapidly. He reaches for his throat, his hands fluttering uselessly, feeling blindly. Finally his head falls forward, his feet still absurdly splayed on the table. It's a relief, when he goes still.

"What now?" Bill says, glaring daggers.

Valerie smiles, her eyes alight with mischief.

"We open all the doors and windows. If you can get back to the mainland alive, you get to keep all the insane amounts of money you didn't actually earn and go on living your selfish, useless lives."

"What's the catch?"

She struggles to keep a straight face. "The catch is that we all know damn well there's only one way off this island."

Valerie nods, and the pink-clad servants open the floor-to-ceiling windows, letting in a rush of wild, welcome sea air. The door to the main hallway is opened, as is the one that Dez assumes must go to the kitchen, where Mr. Rose once kept watch. Chairs scrape as the Ruskins stand and push away from the heavy table. Dez is frozen in place watching James abandon his own wheelchair-bound mother to sprint out the kitchen door, followed by his uncle Frank, who's not quite as nimble.

"Come on," Bill barks, and Dez isn't sure who he's talking to, but he grabs Marie's hand. Her Manolo slingback heels have almost no purchase on the marble, and she kicks them off as he tugs her toward the hallway door.

Patrick stands, and so Dez stands, uncertain what she's supposed to do. She doesn't know this place. She isn't guilty of any Ruskin sins, unless two unhappy days of their hospitality counts. She'd like to throw herself at Valerie's feet and beg for asylum, but not while she's holding a straight razor and grinning at the blood dripping off the table.

"Come on," Patrick says, just like his father, voice low, and when he runs, Dez tears her eyes away from Valerie and follows him. Like Marie, she's already kicked off her shoes, leaving them under the table.

Instead of heading for the doors, Patrick runs to one of the windows, passes through, and pauses briefly as she navigates over the low sill. "Can you run?" he asks.

The Versace is a shift, thank God, short and not confining.

"Yes."

"Then hurry."

He takes off at a sprint, doesn't take her hand or look back to check on her. The white shell path is sharp under her feet, but she doesn't care. Before today, Dez had never seen a dead body. Now she has seen two, has smelled the sudden stench that seeps out when a dead man shits his tuxedo pants. She quickly realizes that Patrick is running for the dock, but he slows down as it becomes obvious that the boat isn't tied there. It's floating out in the ocean, halfway between the Island and all the cars parked on the mainland.

"Fuck!" Patrick barks. He jogs to the edge of the dock and gazes down at layer upon layer of sharp gray shells.

"Look," Dez says, stepping up beside him and pointing at the waves.

Uncle Frank is out there, swimming in long, elegant strokes that don't match the paunchy old man she saw at dinner. He had maybe a minute's head start on them, but he has apparently decided to dive right in and paddle for the ship.

"He tried out for the Olympics a long time ago," Patrick says as he paces back and forth, watching. "Almost got there. Shit! If he can make it to the boat, maybe he'll come back for the rest of us..."

He trails off.

The Ruskins don't seem like heroes.

They're not banding together, helping one another out.

This man just watched his brother die, didn't even pause to help his widow or anyone else. He just ran.

Frank isn't flagging, his strokes certain and strong. The boat floats calmly; the motor isn't even on. Maybe the servants just pulled up the anchor and cut it loose so no one could reach it. If Frank can just make it to the ladder hanging off the side of the boat —

But no.

Pink figures appear on the big, white prow, along the benches where Dez recently sat sipping champagne and dreaming about her future.

They're carrying tall white plastic buckets, and as Frank nears, one servant draws up the ladder while the others upend the buckets into the frothing waves. Red liquid globs out, splashing into the dark blue water around Frank, who stops swimming to slap at his face. Chunks of meat cling to his balding head.

"What are they doing? What are they — oh fuck — they didn't..." Patrick murmurs like he's watching a horror movie instead of a family member.

Uncle Frank must realize what's happening, too, as he redoubles his effort to get on the boat. The ladder is up, but he paddles toward the back, where maybe there's something, anything to climb up, because now that the water around him is red with blood and viscera, the local ocean life is responding with pleasure.

First one fin appears, cutting a sharp curve around Frank, then another. They're big, sleek, gray things, and Dez wishes she cared more about biology so she would know what she's watching.

"Are there sharks around the Island?" she asks quietly.

Patrick stands beside her, likewise transfixed. His hand finds hers, his fingers desperately grasping for something to hold onto.

"Lots of sharks," he confirms. "Bull sharks, tiger sharks, black tips. They clock a great white around here every year. Her name is Sally."

Frank reaches for the yacht, and his hands scrabble for purchase on the sleek white hull, leaving pink stains from all the chum in the water around him. There is nothing to grab onto, no handholds or edges, just perfectly glossy white. As he moves around the boat, desperately reaching and sliding back down, Dez realizes that she can't look away, that there's something magical and transfixing about watching the inevitable approach of death.

There's nothing she can do.

Literally nothing.

She has no phone, no weapon, no power. She can barely swim, but even the strongest swimmer can't outrun one shark, much less a dozen.

Uncle Frank is about to learn.

The first one knocks him sideways, his arms flailing as his tiny, tinny scream echoes over the water. There is no other sound but the pounding surf and the gentle wind and an old man being eaten alive by ancient behemoths older than trees.

"Look away," Patrick says, trying to pull her close as if this is gallant and brave. Dez lets him tug her near, and he clings to her, his chest rising and falling and rising and falling as she watches past his arm, transfixed by the dark water churning, by the empty, reaching hands, by the gray fins clashing and swirling in a frenzy until the surface of the sea is deep burgundy.

And then Frank is gone, and everything goes still.

A single black shoe bobs up to float amidst the gore.

Dez looks up at the ship and sees a line of men in pink staring down, doing nothing, the impersonal sun flashing off their rose-gold sunglasses.

12

"So we can't take the boat," Dez says. Her hair whips around her face as the sun-kissed wind swirls around her bare legs. She shivers, but not from the temperature. She can't stop staring at the boat, at the mainland beyond as it shimmers, spring green against the robin's-egg sky. If not for the bloodied water, it might be an image from a postcard.

Wish you were here.

"Where can we hide?" she asks Patrick.

He doesn't answer; he can only tremble, likewise transfixed by the boat. Perhaps it seemed reachable a few moments ago, but now Dez understands that it's just a mirage, an illusion, a temptation.

An invitation to suicide.

Nothing is safe now.

This bastion of an island, so carefully hidden and protected, is now a dead end.

"Patrick!"

He shakes his head, looks down at her like he's never seen her before.

"What?"

"Where can we hide?" Her mind is going a mile a minute, a roach looking for the next shadow into which to scuttle. "Or get weapons? Where's the closest place?"

It's as if Patrick is thawing out, his eyes bouncing everywhere as he comes back online from wherever he went while watching his uncle get torn to shreds.

"Weapons. The stable. The — the farrier. There are tools. Hammers."

Dez does not want to go back to the stables; the monstrous horses are malevolent enough when there aren't also people trying to kill her. And yet she thinks he must be right. It's a little away from the house, so maybe fewer people will be congregated inside. And there will be dark spaces: the stalls, the hayloft. The sun will begin to set soon. At night, they'll be at a disadvantage. *She'll* be at a disadvantage. She's the only person here who doesn't know this island intimately. She still hasn't seen all of it.

Patrick nods as if trying to convince himself that the stables are the right choice. He casts one last longing look over his shoulder toward the unreachable yacht and starts walking. The white shell path crunches under his dress shoes, and Dez winces, realizing that they must be easy pickings out here. Patrick is the tallest thing around, and any servants on the hunt holding a knife might see them in the open and end them.

And yet — well, they could've kept the doors and windows shut and killed everyone in the ballroom. Valerie had the gun, everyone had a weapon, but they were allowed to run away.

They were all but invited to escape.

There must be some reason.

Dez is certain she doesn't want to know what it is.

She just wants to leave and never come back.

To think — she went to all this trouble just for five minutes with Marie Caulfield-Ruskin, and she still hasn't been introduced to her.

If she wasn't running for her life, Dez would almost think Marie was avoiding her on purpose.

But wait —

"Didn't you say your mom and brother were working when we arrived?"

Patrick doesn't even turn back to look at her. "Yes. So?"

"So that must mean they have an internet connection. I mean, she runs a magazine. It's not like they were filling out forms with a pencil."

"There's a wired connection in the upstairs office."

How doesn't he get it? Is he really that stupid?

"So we need to get up there and call for help. You can do it from Facetime, Zoom, Skype."

He turns back to look at her as realization dawns. "Yes. Yes! So we'll get weapons, then sneak inside and call for help. There's a panic room."

Of course there is.

He holds a finger to his lips as they near the stables, and she angrily points at his massive shoes, which crunch with every step. The horses aren't in the field, and Dez is grateful that not only are the galloping assholes not revealing that she and Patrick are here by whinnying maniacally at them, but also that she's not going to face those giant teeth again.

As they tiptoe up the path, Dez places each bare foot carefully, wincing at the pain, straining to hear any noise from within the big pink barn. If there were servants on the boat, surely there are servants stationed here, waiting to round up any Ruskins like rogue cattle? Someone could just sit at the barn doors and start shooting. There is no sneaking up on the stables, no way to approach that can't be seen if someone is on the lookout. This island was designed to expose trespassers.

Patrick slips in the open door and flattens himself against the wall like some kind of idiot James Bond, and Dez follows, grateful for the much softer sawdust under her bare feet and the solid feel of the wood boards at her back. It's cooler in the barn, quiet and calm, clean and simple in black and white; she could almost pretend she's not currently living in a nightmare and is instead in a Joanna Gaines commercial. At least she feels far less exposed than she felt outside. She is a little mouse who has found a hidey-hole, and she takes her first deep breath in what feels like years.

But then Patrick tenses beside her, and she hears it, too.

Horses, stamping their hooves.

People, murmuring to the horses.

The sound of ropes tightening.

Something is happening.

"You can't do this," someone says — a low, husky voice Dez now recognizes.

Grandmother.

"Why not?" someone else responds — a young woman.

Patrick sneaks through the stable, sticking to the dark edges. Curious noses poke over stall doors, and he ignores them; Dez stays well away from the sharp teeth behind those velvety lips. When Patrick stops by a closed door and mutters, "Shit," Dez freezes. There's a lock hanging there, a shiny new silver padlock — the kind that needs a key.

"The room with the hammers?" she guesses.

"Obviously." He looks at her like it's her fault, like if she just hadn't said the words out loud, it wouldn't be true.

She does not like the look.

He hasn't looked at her like that before, and she sees shades of his father in it.

It's a good thing she doesn't actually love him, much less like him.

He shakes his head and ducks down, hurrying toward a bigger space up ahead. Dez casts a desperate glance around the barn, noting how extremely clean it is, how there are no random buckets of junk anywhere, nothing hanging on nails, no blunt force instruments just waiting to be grabbed like they always are in movies.

This is what the Ruskins get for demanding constant cleanliness. All their potential weapons are neatly locked away, completely out of reach. Just like their kind of wealth, to the rest of the world.

She hears movement nearby and looks up to find someone peering at her from an empty stall — Will and Genevieve.

Genevieve is a wreck, she's clearly been crying and her sequined dress is torn, but Will looks determined. He makes a hammer motion at Patrick, and Patrick makes a 'yeah, I know, I'd like a hammer, too, you asshole' motion back at his eldest brother.

"That hurts," Grandmother complains, somewhere up ahead.

"That's kind of the point," a younger woman answers.

Patrick gestures with his chin, and Dez follows him up the long row of stalls. Will duck-walks behind them, leaving Genevieve behind. When Dez looks back into the stall, the other woman is curled in a ball in the back corner, her eyes shining in the dark as she rocks back and forth.

Oh, God, Dez thinks.

Her children.

Her children… that she and Will have chosen to abandon to save their own skins.

The little boys must be somewhere in that gigantic house, being watched over by the servants who have proven they're out for blood.

They might already be dead.

Dez thinks about the big buckets of chum the men in pink threw into the water, gallons of blood and chunks of —

Surely not.

What kind of person would do that?

She has to — her mind — she can't —

She has to focus.

"Valerie, *ow*, stop! Stop that right now! What do you hope to gain? Is it money you want? Part of the property? Here. Take my diamonds. They're Cartier. But you know that already, don't you?"

There's a big, wide doorway up ahead, sized for people on horseback to pass easily into the grand space beyond. Dez doesn't know the word for it — it's a sort of large, enclosed ring for horses to be ridden around in circles on the soft, gray dirt. And in the middle of it, Grandmother sits in her wheelchair, still in her black formal gown with her double strand diamond necklace, black hose on her spindly legs and elegant black heels sitting primly side by side. A servant in her pink dress is fussing with something tied to the old woman's arm —

A rope.

The last of four ropes.

One tied to each wrist, one to each ankle.

"You think a necklace will win me over, Grandmother? That we'll all just go back to the way things were because you throw jewels at us? This is so much bigger than that. You let all this happen. You watched it. The men I can almost understand. But you? They took your daughters. Your *babies*. Didn't that make you furious?"

Grandmother sits calmly, her gnarled hands clutching the arms of her wheelchair.

"I had babies," the old woman says reproachfully. "Two beautiful sons."

"But that's not all you had," Valerie says.

She steps behind the wheelchair and gently lowers another rope over the dandelion puff of the old woman's hair, settling it around her neck, right above the diamonds.

Only then does Dez notice the five horses waiting impatiently, stomping their huge black feet in the gray dirt, each one wearing a saddle. And attached to each saddle, a rope.

Grooms in pink livery hold the horses at their heads, speaking calmly to their charges, lead ropes in one hand and whips in the other. More servants wait around the edges of the arena, where there are bleachers for hundreds of spectators, spectators who would have no reason to be on a private island. The audience is silent, curious.

Eager.

"I know someone is watching," Valerie says, stepping away from the wheelchair. She tugs the pink kerchief off her light brown hair and unties the knot. "And I know you know why our precious grandmother has to die today. She let it happen. She watched it happen. For generations, she bought her diamonds and made her perfumes and lipsticks and bred her polo ponies. She loves these horses more than she loves her own children. Including the ones she threw away like garbage. When she could walk, this is where she always was, cultivating only the finest bloodlines. And that's why today, we'll let the horses decide. Will they run toward her, to repay all the love she's given them?" She considers the kerchief in her hands, running it through her fingers. "Or will they run away from the monster she truly is?"

Valerie looks to each groom where he holds the lead rope of a horse that's fighting to be free. Each man nods. Valerie smiles.

She backs away from the wheelchair, away from the old woman.

"You don't have to do this," Grandmother says. "Name your price — "

"Your head."

Valerie picks up a long stick from the ground; it has a whip on the end of it, and she whoops as she flicks it at the nearest horse's rump. Each of the grooms uses his whip, goading his horse to run away from the center of the ring.

Dez can only stare as the old woman's body rises out of the wheelchair, pulled in five different directions as she screams, a low, animal moan. Tension pulls each limb, jerking her back and forth in all directions like a doll in a hurricane, her neck pulled sideways, her withered legs spread unnaturally, her eyes closed like if she just pretends this isn't happening, it won't. One arm leaves the socket with a wet crack, and Dez thinks about her mother deboning a chicken. A hip pops with a loud snap and a sharp intake of breath, stopping the old woman's cry for the merest moment before it ratchets up to a throat-shredding desperate scream. There is the longest, strangest moment as the old woman is held there, buoyed, flying, a perfect star.

And then her head pops off, the horse freed to gallop away, dragging it briefly before the rope slips off the ragged neck and leaves two strands of diamonds sparkling against the blood-spattered dirt.

13

Four horses are still straining frantically, wildly, savagely in their own directions, perhaps not meaning to pull the rest of the body apart but doing it nevertheless in their haste to escape. What's left of Grandmother looks like a prop, like a mannequin, like a prom dress stuffed with straw, except for all the blood.

Patrick has seen enough. He takes off down the long hallway at a full-on run, as if he's forgotten Dez completely. Will follows him, but Genevieve stays where she is, hunched up out of sight, shaking, surrounded by green clumps of horse shit. The servants who aren't tending the horses begin to walk toward the line of stalls, but not as if they're hunting the Ruskins hiding here. Dez knows she can't trust Patrick and his brother, knows that this is life or death and Patrick has chosen himself, but she also knows that he has knowledge of this island, this estate, that she doesn't. He'll know where to hide, and if there really are any weapons stashed away, he'll find them and probably be better at using them.

She runs.

Now that she knows what the white shell path feels like on bare feet, she dreads the moment she's out of the soft sawdust of the stables. Horses squeal and teeth snap from stall doors as she runs past, as if they are aroused by the blood in the air and can sense that she's not supposed to be here, like they can smell her peasant lineage rising with the sweat of her fear.

Twilight is falling outside, but she sees Patrick and Will sprinting toward the garden, so she follows. They stick to the paths like programmed robots, but she is desperate and not trained to respect this place; she cuts through the softer dirt, leaping over the bigger bushes and trampling the flowers, avoiding the thorny roses. She wonders what will happen to Genevieve, if she's too scared to move or has some other plan, but then she hears a scream from the stables, a high-pitched call of, "No! Please, no!" and decides she's not going to turn around and find out.

Patrick and Will skid around a corner, changing direction, and Dez sees a man in pink walking toward them along the path, a long and jagged fish knife in his hand. The brothers are headed toward the pool now, and Dez angles to follow them. Something is different, something is *wrong*, her animal brain is clamoring for her attention, and then she understands why. She sees the smoke before she smells it, a single gray column rising lazily into the periwinkle sky. Patrick and his brother change course again; another man in pink is walking toward them from the house, holding a pair of gardening shears.

It's almost as if…

They're being herded?

Dez leaps over a row of flowers, wincing as her dress tears. For years, she's longed to get her hands on a Versace, and now she has one, and it's being destroyed by the simple act of surviving. Couture is not designed for struggle, for running, for riding the thin line between life and death. It's meant for swanning around a marble room, champagne in hand without a care in the world, for sitting delicately on the edge of a velvet chaise. The thick fabric is just holding her back now. When she looks over her shoulder toward the stables, she sees another figure in pink moving toward them.

Now she's certain — they are buffalo being run into a canyon, mice caught in a maze. She puts on a burst of speed, glad that she's kept up with her cardio. If she's going to die here, they've got to catch her first, and they'll have to get through Patrick and Will because she's going to hide behind them.

They're at the fancier, more formal pool now, so innocently blue and inviting, a place that can offer no safety. She weaves around lounge chairs and tables and umbrellas and slows as she sees Patrick and Will stopped up ahead by a pergola, turning back to back, hands up like maybe someone sent them to boxing camp when they were kids and gave them too much praise.

Ha. As if the two pampered men have any chance when facing off with dozens of armed servants.

When she looks behind her, she sees more pink-clad servants, the noose tightening. There is nowhere to go, nowhere to run. Dez is trapped, too. She limps toward Patrick and Will, her feet sore as hell, staring at the smoke billowing out of the pizza oven under the beautiful, flower-covered pergola. The fire within is roaring hot, the inside of the oven glowing cherry red. A chill goes up her spine. This fire is not accidental.

"What do you want?" Will says, his voice a deep bark as if he's playacting being his father. "Money? Investments? I don't know if Mom and Dad —" he swallows hard. "I don't know who's left, but if I'm the oldest, I'll sign over whatever you want. Just let me go."

Not us.

Not let *us* go.

Me.

Dez begins to see why Genevieve took her chances without her husband.

More and more servants appear, creating a wall of pink around the three of them. Dez is only slightly comforted by the fact that none of the weapons they hold are covered in blood. They all wear those same rose-gold sunglasses, their eyes hidden behind mirrors, the women's hair under kerchiefs. Except Valerie. She's the only one with a name Dez has heard, and she wears neither kerchief nor glasses. Her pink dress is the only one with bloodstains. The gun is a bulky form in her apron pocket, and if Dez can see Patrick and Will eyeing it with the desperate hunger of a bulldog staring at a grill, then so can everyone else.

"Let you go?" Valerie says, as if this is some novel collection of words that carry no meaning. "As if you just deserve to walk away and live a full life. As if all we want is money and power. You just can't imagine wanting anything else, can you?"

"Val, come on. You know me. We grew up together. What are you going to do, kill me?" Will says, putting on the full

Frat Boy Suck-up Show that Dez has seen dozens of times at school, the boys so confident that they think they can fool any girl into bed and out of assault charges, the same boys ready to call them bitches if they don't immediately swoon and spread. Dez is outraged to see how readily he shifts to selfish swagger, completely ignoring the fact that his children are missing and his wife's screams will never stop haunting her.

"Oh, I do know you, Willie. You know who else knows you? Margaret."

Dez is watching Will's face when that name drops, and she sees the color drain from his tanned skin.

"Don't bring Margaret into this." Will's hands go up, his shoulders rising to his ears. Patrick steps away from him, which is also toward Dez, but this action is purely defensive. He's desperate to escape Will's orbit.

Valerie looks to one of the pink-clad women. "Do you want me to do it?" she asks softly.

The girl — the woman — is not the same as the others. Dez hasn't seen her before — she would've noticed. Whereas the other women have bare arms under their short-sleeved uniform dresses, Margaret is wearing a turtleneck that covers her from chin to wrists, plus thin cotton gloves — all the exact same, correct shade of pink, of course. The light brown hair under her kerchief is stringy and patchy. And her face is…

God, the poor girl.

Under the sunglasses, her skin bears the shiny, twisted pink of burn marks, her lips crookedly quirked up on one side. She takes a deep breath, and a little sob breaks free.

"You don't have to," Valerie says. "It's up to you."

"No." Margaret's voice is much, much older than she is and suggests she smokes three packs a day, deep and ragged and tired. "No, this one is mine." She steps out of the circle, and the girls on either side of her touch her shoulders gently in support.

Will is panicky, his eyes shooting everywhere. He stumbles back, bumps into Patrick, but Patrick shoves him off and moves away. When Will looks to Dez, she no longer sees a successful businessman, a celebrated philanthropist and angel investor, a father, a husband. She sees a frightened little boy who knows he's in trouble, who can see the punishment coming and will do anything to avoid it. Sensing his desperation, the circle of servants tightens, leaving no gaps. Knives and hammers and shears shine, and the men look like they'd happily beat him to death, if asked. Before tonight's dinner, she couldn't tell the male servants apart; they all have the same bland smile, the same hidden eyes. Now they all share the same primal rage.

"Kneel," Margaret says quietly as she stares at Will.

"What?" He licks his lips. "What?"

She steps up to him, close enough to touch.

"I want you to kneel."

"I don't—"

"Do it!" one of the men barks.

Valerie pulls the gun from her pocket. "Do it," she repeats with dangerous softness.

Will still thinks he can escape somehow. He stares from one servant to the next as if looking for an open window. "Thomas? Henry? Come on, guys. You know how it is—"

One of the men he's addressing lumbers forward, a chef's knife of elegant Damascus steel gleaming in his hand. "We know how it *was*. Now kneel."

"Just do it," Patrick mutters.

The man with the knife takes a threatening step forward, and still Will stands. Dez doesn't know if he's just that accustomed to being in power or if he really is that stupid.

"Kneel or I'll shoot you in the leg," Valerie says, making a show of checking the clip on her gun before sliding it back home, the loudest noise on the Island other than crackling flames. "Or Thomas can slice your ankles, just like Gage in *Pet Sematary*. Remember how much that used to scare you? Either way, it's going to hurt."

Will looks at Patrick and Dez like they've betrayed him somehow and kneels. There's something disturbing about a man in an expensive tux on his knees, the strange juxtaposition of power and powerlessness. He looks up at Valerie, then at Margaret.

"What now?" he asks with a sneer.

Oh, how he hates being forced to look up at the servants.

Margaret stands before him, his head at her waist. He does not look up at her now; he looks anywhere else, as if he can't stand the sight of her.

"Beg me for forgiveness."

Will's shoulders hunch up around his head, his hands in fists, a little boy working up to a tantrum. "I don't know what you want me to say."

Valerie steps behind him, puts the gun's muzzle to the back of his head, execution style. "Let me help you, then. *Margaret, I'm sorry that I pushed you into the pizza oven on my fourteenth birthday because you accidentally burned my pizza. I was a selfish little prick who never had to learn the word* no, *or that there are consequences for my actions. I'm sorry your hair caught fire and your face and hands and arms got burned, and that the family refused to send you to a doctor on the mainland or get you plastic surgery, so you just had to make do with basic first aid. I'm sorry that for the last twelve years, I've pretended like you didn't exist.* Does that about cover it?"

"He should also apologize for what he did when he was thirteen," Margaret says. "When I was still pretty."

The gun presses into Will's head like an unwilling kiss, and he leans away from it, eyes closed and leaking tears.

"I was just a kid," he whispers. "Thirteen is just a kid."

Margaret reaches into her dress pocket and pulls out a little bottle of lighter fluid. She sprays it on Will's head, and he flinches away and tries to wipe it off, but she keeps on squirting it all over his shoulders, his chest, every part of him until the bottle is empty.

"What the fuck?" he says, blinking as he rubs at his eyes.

Margaret reaches for a — whatever they use to get pizza out of pizza ovens, a flat metal shovel on a long stick. She shoves it into the open oven and expertly pulls out a pizza that's burned to a crisp and still on fire.

"I was just a kid, too. And I don't forgive you."

She swings the pizza toward Will, throwing it at him, and it touches his hair like a benediction and sends flames leaping upward. He screams and bats at his head with his hands, but they, too, are covered in lighter fluid. The fire spreads up the arms of his tuxedo, over his chest, down his legs to the puddle of lighter fluid all around him, and he is screaming and screaming and screaming as he wobbles to his feet and runs. There's no way he can see, no way his brain can be working, but he grew up here, and he knows where the pool is. He runs toward it, every inch of him crackling with orange flames, but the line of pink-clad servants doesn't falter. A woman holds out a long chef's knife, and he runs right into it, and it sticks in his belly, and he turns around to try a different direction. Blood drips from the knife handle as he charges away, directly into a pitchfork. The man holding the handle gives a mighty shove, sending Will sprawling on his back.

The screams — they don't stop — they are forever — Dez can see Will's face now, his open mouth, his open eyes burning, everything burning, burning, burning. Will thrashes on his back like a bug that just won't die. The pitchfork stuck in his belly falls over, leaving blood gushing from four wounds on the once-white shirt, the knife quivering like a question mark amidst the flames.

"Just kill him," Patrick says, voice rough. "Make the screaming stop."

"No," Margaret says, her rusty voice firmer now. She is still holding the pizza shovel. "I want to hear it. I want to watch it happen."

The servants are transfixed, watching Will thrash and flail on the ground, leaving burned black streaks on the pavers. The air smells of fresh barbecue, and Dez's gorge rises.

Patrick grabs the fallen pitchfork and runs at the circle of servants, swinging it as he shouts with unintelligible rage. The servants step aside, and when he barges through, Dez follows him.

Will is still screaming.

The servants do not give chase.

This is not an escape, Dez thinks.

This is just another part of their plan.

14

Pitchfork in hand, not looking back, Patrick runs for the house. Dez follows, wishing she could plug her ears. Unlike Margaret, she doesn't want to hear the screams. She just wants to get away.

Patrick doesn't look back, doesn't even seem aware of her anymore. He is simply a hunted animal going to ground, fending only for itself. He throws open a side door, and Dez catches it and steps into the echoing, air-conditioned space of a hallway, with its gleaming marble floors and wafting scent of roses. There are signs of a struggle — a plinth overturned, a crystal vase broken and spilling water and flowers, a rug that is rumpled after years of lying flat. Patrick no longer stands with the ease and confidence of the Finance Bro he so resembles. He's nearly crouching, knees bent, ready to run, holding the pitchfork defensively, its tines black with fire and red with blood. He's thinking, and he's not doing a good job of it.

"Is there any place the servants don't know about?" Dez asks him.

He whips around, brandishing the pitchfork before realizing it's just her. A quick scowl confirms he wishes it wasn't. But then he recomposes his face, gives her a little smile.

He's realizing I might be of use, Dez thinks.

Probably as a human shield.

She knows now he can't be trusted.

"The servants know everything we know," he says, like she's an idiot.

"Then where's a good place to hide? Where wouldn't they look? Should we try that panic room? Or contacting the mainland from the office?"

He's breathing through his nose, chest heaving as the gears in his brain turn. "The panic room is on the other side of the house — the other wing. The wired connection, too. But there are lots of places to hide in the attic. It's all storage, a hundred years of shit nobody wanted to drag to the mainland. Might still be some weapons up there, like a fireplace poker or something. It's huge. And there's a stairway to the other wing."

Dez nods. "Let's go."

Patrick cocks his head, listening, but there are no sounds. Respecting that silence — and the other people who might be listening — he walks as quietly as he can in his rigid black shoes. Dez is still barefoot, and she's going to swipe the first pair of usable shoes she can in case they have to go outside again — the ten-year-old boy is probably around her size. She's aware that the soles of her feet are destroyed, bruised and scratched and cut by the shell path, but she's also aware that there's enough adrenaline pumping through her system to quiet the pain of all but the worst sort of wound. At least she doesn't leave bloody footprints on the marble as she tiptoes along behind the idiot she thought she was using.

It's a relief to make it to the stairs — not the grand stairwell that would reveal them to anyone looking, and not the cramped, twisting servants' stairwell that would now feel like a trap, but a third one that is plushly carpeted. It seems like it was specifically made for the family's comfort and ease.

Halfway up the stairs, Dez hears a door open down below, and Patrick picks up speed. The carpet muffles their steps, thank God, and then they're on the second floor. Patrick freezes, listening, checking that the hallway is clear before hurrying out. He doesn't wait for Dez, but she doesn't expect him to. He darts over to a door that she would take for one of the suites, except it turns out to be another set of carpeted stairs leading upward. She pauses in the open doorway but doesn't hear anything happening on this floor.

Patrick is already out of view, and Dez silently shuts the door to catch up with him. The stairs open on a vast space lit only by the eaves and some vents. The ceiling is lower here than downstairs but still high enough for Patrick to walk without hunching over. Seabirds cry outside, and the ocean's pounding is back, surrounding Dez like a great beast's heartbeat. Will's screams have stopped, or perhaps the wind has stolen them away. A lone horse whinnies, and Dez shivers.

There aren't really any aisles among the hulking piles of boxes and the ghostly shapes of old furniture covered in dusty white cloths like forgotten plague victims. It seems as if things were dragged up here, pushed within, and abandoned where they lay. This would suggest to Dez that the oldest things would be the farthest from this door — or the other door Patrick mentioned. In the center, maybe.

She tiptoes after Patrick, shuffling her feet carefully so she won't step on a nail or a dead rat or a rusty staple. And so she won't make a noise that might be heard by those below. She has never longed for her phone with so much desperation, not only for its ability to contact civilization, but for the simple pleasure of a bit of light in the darkness, which she entirely takes for granted in her regular life.

"Where's the other door?" she whispers.

"Shh!"

She'd like to point out that his shushing her is louder than her whispering, but that would only make more noise. She goes silent but does not appreciate it. In the crepuscular light of the shadowy space, she can barely see him hold up one finger and point to the opposite corner of the attic. The other door.

Scritch.

Somewhere in the vast space, there is a sound.

A small sound.

Someone moving, the smallest shift of weight.

Patrick and Dez both freeze.

"That's my brother," a male voice whispers angrily.

"Shh!" a female voice hisses back.

"Anthony?" Patrick takes a few steps toward where he heard the sound.

He edges around stacked wood chairs, steps over a cardboard box labeled *OLD TOYS*. There's a creak up ahead and to the right, and a shape appears in the aisle, an arm in a black sleeve beckoning to them. They find Anthony and Christiane hiding under a card table with a cloth over it. It's almost comical — the second most powerful person at *Nouveau*, Marie's number two man and chief financial officer, is tucked up under an old table, cross-legged in his tux like a little boy who doesn't want to go to bed after a party. Christiane is sprawled beside him, one hand on her belly, her mascara streaking down her face. Dez can see these details because there's a small electric candle sitting on the floor. That warm, weak light is the most welcome thing she's encountered in a while.

"Move over," Patrick says, preparing to slide under the table, his pitchfork on the ground beside him.

"No way. Find somewhere else." Anthony moves over, taking up as much room as possible. "We need to spread out, not cluster up."

"Then why did you call us over here?"

"So you wouldn't make the kind of noise that would draw the servants up here."

"Oh, God, you're both so loud," Christiane whisper-moans, one hand on her stomach, eyes closed as if she's trying to make a nightmare go away. "I think I'm in labor. What do we do?"

Patrick ignores that, just like everyone is ignoring the fact that these parents are not with their only child, or even looking for him. "Do you even know what's been happening out there?"

"I saw what happened to Mr. Rose and Grandfather, and I know that my best bet is to hide here until someone escapes, or help arrives. Go find your own table." When Patrick doesn't move, Anthony lifts a foot and kicks at his younger brother's shin.

Over the sound of their petulant scuffle, Dez hears footsteps coming up the stairs. She gets on her hands and knees and shuffles along, looking for her own place to hide. She's not going to waste time trying to fight her way under their already crowded table.

There's an open space up ahead, the boxes and furniture pushed together and piled up like a wall, almost as if making a hidden room in the back of the attic. There are open shelves built into the walls here, each one covered in old board games and stacks of *National Geographic*s, with cabinets underneath. When Dez opens one of the cabinets, she finds more shelves, deeper ones, perhaps made for records but now mostly empty, and she slides in feet-first on her belly and gently closes the door once she's all the way in. It feels absolutely wretched in here, dust and dirt clinging to her bare legs and thighs and feet, her dress riding up stiffly around her neck. Something tickles her ankle, and she couldn't reach it even if she wanted to. Spiders are the least of her worries right now.

With no warning, overhead lights come on, and Dez blinks against the sudden brightness that slices in between the cabinet doors and two empty holes that must've once secured door handles. She can hear the footsteps now — lots of them. If she leans forward and squints, she can just barely see what's happening in the open area outside through one of the drilled holes.

"Olly olly oxen free!" a voice calls — Valerie, Dez thinks. "Come on out, Anthony. We know you're up here."

The footsteps are spread around the attic labyrinth, winding through the stacks, taking their time with quiet menace. Someone places something in the open space with a heavy thump, and Dez sees one of those big plastic bins that people buy for storing artificial Christmas trees or whatever, maybe four or five feet long and two feet tall. It's a heavy, industrial black, just sitting on the dusty boards. There are several more thumps, and Dez isn't sure what the servants have placed around the tub, but she's pretty sure it's not going to be good for Anthony.

"There you are," Valerie says. "Are you going to come out, or do we have to drag you?"

"Fuck you," Anthony barks.

"Drag it is."

Dez hears scuffling noises as Anthony is pulled out from under his table. She hears nothing from Patrick or Christiane, and wonders if they've also been caught or if they scattered in time to avoid Anthony's fate. Anthony is fighting his captors, but the servants must have him in hand. He's not a huge man, doesn't seem terribly muscular, but it sounds like he's struggling to get free and failing, kicking over chairs and boxes every step of the way with the chaos of a cat that doesn't want to go in the bath.

"What is this?" he says once he's in the open area. Dez can see the heels of his shiny black shoes, the cobweb-strung hems of his black tuxedo pants. "What do you want?"

"It's so funny." Dez sees Valerie's pink Keds walk around the plastic tub. Those shoes were pristine the first time she saw them, but they wear rusty red stains now. "Everyone keeps asking what we want, like they think we're just doing this for money. Like we can be bought. Like they think if they just offer us enough, we'll let them go."

"I can make you a very attractive offer, I have access to — "

She shoves him, and he tumbles backward into the black plastic tub, his arms and legs flailing out like a turtle on its back. It would be almost funny if Valerie didn't have the gun pointed at his face.

"Here's the offer. Apologize to Ed and Leo."

Anthony goes quiet. He stops squirming. Dez wishes she could see his face, but she can guess what it looks like — just like Will's when he was told to apologize to Margaret.

The Ruskins, it would appear, have a lot to apologize for.

"We were just boys," Anthony finally says. His voice is high, nervous. "Just boys messing around."

A man's yacht shoes appear in Dez's vision, one of the male servants standing over Anthony. To the side, out of Dez's view, there is a heavy thump like a bag being emptied, and gray powder fills the air; she has to hold in a desperate cough. She hears water being poured, the gloppy sound of something thick being stirred.

"We were just boys," a man muses. "But we had to do what you told us. *You* were messing around. *We* were victims. We wanted to say no, but you gagged us. Told us to hold still. To not move a muscle. To close our eyes and not look at you. To never tell a soul."

More water is poured. Whatever is being stirred sounds thicker now, like mud.

"Do you remember how much you made me bleed?" a different man says. "You just left me there. The doctor had to stitch me up." A sob escapes the man. "You said it was my fault for making you hard. It never healed right, Tony."

"I'm sorry," Anthony Ruskin says, too quickly. "I'm sorry, okay? I was young and stupid. I thought — I thought you were into it."

"People who are into it don't need to be tied to the bed," Valerie says as one of the men tries not to cry and fails. "The bed you set up here, in the corner. The old twin, with its four posters."

"I'm sorry," Anthony says. Then, louder, "I'm sorry, okay? You win! You can have everything! I'll sign whatever you want! Just take it!"

"What do you want, Ed? Leo?" Valerie asks with sly malice.

"I want him to hold still. I want him to never tell a soul."

There's a scrape, and Dez sees two of the men pouring a huge bucket of something heavy into the tub with Anthony, on top of Anthony. She can smell it now — the concrete. She remembers it distinctly from when they were doing construction at the hotel and her mom had to shower off the powder every night. They pick up another bucket and pour that in, too, and Anthony is trying to get out of the tub, but it's an awkward shape, and it's deep, and Ed and Leo keep pushing him back in. There are more bags of emptied concrete, more puffs of powder, more glugging of water, more thick, sloppy stirring.

The servants — they were prepared for this.

Very, very well prepared.

"Christiane!" Anthony screams. "Christiane, help me!"

"Your beard can't help you," Leo says. "Now, open your mouth."

If she moves her head just right, Dez can see a man holding Anthony's hair, pulling it, canting his head back, pinching his nose closed until he's forced to open his mouth. Leo has a pitcher of concrete ready, and he pours it between Anthony's lips in a thick, chunky stream until it spills out down his cheeks. Anthony is choking, gargling, his screams muffled. Leo reaches for the bigger bucket of concrete someone else is mixing, uses a trowel to pick up a thick mound and fill Anthony's throat.

Other servants are pouring concrete into the tub still, and Anthony can't move much, his hands reaching for nothing, his feet kicking impotently.

"Maybe he should close his eyes so he can't see," Valerie suggests.

Ed and Leo share a look, and then Leo rams the concrete-covered trowel into Anthony's left eye.

15

I t's a good thing the concrete mixing makes so much noise, because Dez knows she gasped when the trowel hit home. Anthony Ruskin is barely twitching now, a fountain of thick concrete rising from his mouth, both of his eyes gouged out and leaking gray-tinged blood down his temples. Somewhere deeper into the attic, there's a scuffle, and the sounds Dez hears suggest Christiane has made a run for it. No footsteps follow her. Dez isn't sure whether to find this comforting, that maybe the servants are only after those who actually caused them harm… or if it just means something has been planned for Christiane farther along the timeline. The servants definitely have a plan, and they are executing it. If they want Christiane dead, she will be.

Once Anthony has gone completely still, the servants leave.

"Fuck him," Leo says.

"He deserved every bit of it," Ed says, then Dez hears him spit. They leave together. Dez hopes they found some comfort in what they just did. She never actually officially met Anthony, but she hates him, too.

Valerie is the last one left. Dez can see her shoes standing by the tub. She wonders what the woman is waiting for. She holds her breath as long as she can.

And then Valerie walks away with the calm, measured confidence of a well-fed predator. Dez waits until all the footsteps are gone, then waits a moment more. She hears a box shoved aside deeper into the attic and emerges from the cabinet, slithering out like a giraffe birth, landing in a heap, and scrambling to her feet. Patrick is standing over his dead brother, and it's not a pretty sight. The concrete is hardening around Anthony's body — Dez had no idea the chemical reaction happened so quickly, but she sees several bags labeled 'Quickcrete.' Now his wrists and feet and head stick out of a solid block of gray. It would be better if his head was covered — his face is grotesquely swollen and purple, the concrete making sick bulges in his throat. And his eyes —

Well, if Dez lives through this ordeal, they will haunt her forever.

"It wasn't his fault," Patrick says softly.

Dez does not respond to this.

She's pretty sure it *was* his fault.

She's also pretty sure it doesn't matter now.

She has a better chance of staying alive if she's with Patrick.

He still has a pitchfork, after all.

But wait.

She reaches out and unties the first of Anthony's shoes, slowly, uncertain what Patrick will do.

He slaps her hands away. "Don't you fucking touch him!"

"My feet are bleeding," she says softly. "He has socks — "

"Then go get someone else's fucking socks. He was my brother!"

"He's gone, Patrick. He doesn't need socks anymore."

She puts a comforting hand on his shoulder, and his head drops forward.

And then he hits her.

Something between a slap and a punch: a clumsy, open-handed thing that catches her on the cheekbone.

"Touch him again and I'll kill you myself," he snarls.

She doesn't think he will, but her body is currently in revolt.

No one has ever hit her before.

She is shocked, insulted, hurt, wounded, wants to fall on the ground and clutch her face.

And yet... what she's seen today, all the adrenaline, the pain radiating from her cheekbone.

He *hit* her.

She's furious.

"Hit me again and I'll kill you first," she snarls right back.

She turns on her bare heel and strides out of the attic, doubling back to see if the electric candle is still on the ground under the table, which it is. Her dress doesn't have pockets, because of course it doesn't; if it did, why would women need expensive purses? So she tucks the candle into her bra and heads back to the open space, where she ignores Patrick, who's crying, and grabs an old hoe from an emptied concrete bucket, one of the ones they used to mix the powder with water. A hardening glob of concrete clings to it, but that's fine. Even that can be a weapon.

Without another word to Patrick, she leaves, taking the set of stairs she hasn't used yet. As she'd hoped, it is the one nearest her room, and when she doesn't see anyone in the hall, she goes to her door and listens briefly before slipping inside.

As far as she can tell, no one else has been here since she left it. The first thing she does is go to the sink and drink water, because she knows that human beings can go quite some time without eating and barely any time at all without drinking. The stream is normal at first, the water pressure strong, but then it trickles out to nothing.

The servants have turned off the water supply.

Dez feels like an animal being run to ground by a smarter hunter. She pulls the top off the toilet, reassured that the back tank looks relatively clean and doesn't have visible chemicals in it. If nothing else, she can survive drinking toilet tank water. Next, she goes to her armoire and puts on black yoga pants — Lululemons, bought thrifting — and a black shirt, because it's almost dark now, and she needs every advantage she can get. Socks and sneakers follow, and then she braids her hair back tightly. She searches the room for anything remotely helpful and finds nothing, because who went through her belongings when she arrived?

The servants.

Even her tiny eyebrow scissors and toenail clippers are gone, which she didn't notice until just now.

At least she has shoes.

She knows her socks are going to stick to the abraded soles of her feet, knows the cloth will be crusted to her body with blood, but that's a problem for another day, if she lives to see it.

As she hunts through the bathroom drawers, her attention is caught by her image in the mirror. She looks wild, haunted, terrified, like she's entering into some weird version of *The Hunger Games*. Just a few hours ago, she was applying makeup with the utmost care, spraying on a sample of perfume she can't actually afford, preparing herself to make a good impression on Marie Caulfield-Ruskin and secure her future. Now she doesn't even know if she'll have a future.

In the other room, her door creaks open.

She snatches up the hoe, now a bludgeon with its knob of concrete, and ducks down so she can't be seen in the mirror. She contemplates the best place to hit someone with her weapon so they'll be dead or incapacitated — something she's never thought about before.

The skull, she thinks. *Aim for the eyes.*

"Dez?"

The air leaves her with a whoosh as she realizes it's just Patrick.

For a moment, she thinks she won't answer him. But then she remembers that if it comes down to her or a Ruskin, the servants will likely concentrate on the Ruskin, giving her time to run away in her Nikes.

"You gonna hit me again?" she says, because she no longer has to pretend that she likes him.

"That was an accident. I was — I haven't — I didn't mean to. He's my brother."

130

The most pathetic excuse.

Like that makes it okay to hit a woman.

She stands, hoe in her hands. It's starting to get heavy.

"They took all the weapons. They took my fingernail file," she says.

He glances around her room like he's never been in one of the smaller ones before and finds it lacking. "Yeah. They do that to guests."

"Even when they're not planning on killing everyone?"

The look he gives her suggests he's not the kind of person who appreciates jokes during a massacre.

"For safety. Assassination attempts. That sort of thing." He exhales, runs a hand through his hair. Parts of it are still stuck together by gel. "The panic room. I think we should try there next."

"What makes you think they haven't taken it over?"

"Because when the door locks, a klaxon is supposed to sound. It can be heard all the way on the mainland."

Dez reckons the servants could easily find a way to silence the klaxon; the Ruskins don't strike her as the most tech-savvy people and have likely farmed out every job that feels remotely like work or involves learning anything new. On the other hand...

"Is there water in there?"

"Water, food, electricity, a sat phone."

These are the most beautiful words Dez has ever heard.

"Let's try it. And if that doesn't work, the office?"

He nods and looks around her room critically, noting the Versace dress discarded on the floor, making him frown a little.

Hoe in one hand, she follows him when he leaves. Patrick strides down the center of the hallway in his tux like the concepts of ownership or superiority still apply, the pitchfork in one hand. Dez doesn't walk beside him — she sort of trails behind him. He can go around the corners first.

They don't encounter anyone, and Dez notes that all the doors are still closed. She wonders if any of the Ruskins are taking shelter within, hiding under a bed or inside an armoire. Christiane is still left, as are Bill, Marie, and James, as far as she knows. Genevieve might be, but she doesn't think so. And then there are the children — the three boys. They have to be... somewhere.

She can't think about that now.

Patrick takes the carpeted family stairwell, which puts them in the hallway downstairs. Dez is surprised that he isn't sneaking at all, but then — well, how would that help? There is no place to hide in the hallway. Crouching won't magically provide camouflage. He's a six-foot-two man in a tux carrying a bloody pitchfork. If they're looking for him, they're going to find him.

The soft slap of a rubber-soled shoe sounds on the marble behind them, and Patrick looks over his shoulder and breaks into a run. Dez doesn't have to look before she runs; she knows the sound of Keds when she hears it, and she knows that anyone who wasn't a servant would call out to them instead of chasing them. Patrick's slick shoes slip as he turns the corner, but Dez has her sneakers on and quickly catches up. He slaps a button that looks like it's part of a sconce, and a door that was hidden in the pink paneling swings inward. Patrick doesn't gallantly offer to let her go first; he squeezes in, and she follows. Ahead of them is a small hallway terminating in a door made of thick metal.

Patrick smashes his thumb into a pad by the door...

And nothing happens.

He moves his thumb around several times before pressing a series of numbers on the keypad. There are no beeps, no lights, just a flat black screen.

"Goddammit," he murmurs, and Dez doesn't need to ask why.

Maybe someone is already in there, maybe the servants cut the wires, but either way, the door will not open. There is no handle for this door. It was, after all, designed to keep people on the outside from getting inside.

"Come on," he says.

The secret passage takes a hard left into a narrow hallway that's dark and dusty. Patrick has to turn sideways to squeeze through. Little darts of light pierce the shadows, and Dez recognizes peepholes that must be behind portraits in the hallway. If she wasn't about to be murdered, she would be delighted. Had she been born wealthy, she would definitely invest in a secret hallway with peepholes, plus a bookshelf that spins when the right statue is tilted. The Ruskins really don't use their money to properly produce joy.

She briefly pauses at the next set of holes and goes up on her tiptoes to look out. She sees a sprawling living room in shades of pink and ivory, the sort of place that's meant to look inviting but is so fancy that no one in the family would actually spend time there. She imagines no butts have ever touched that perfect, fluffy sofa.

The light is blocked, and then gray-blue eyes are staring into hers.

She gasps and scurries after Patrick.

Now there are sounds in the secret passageway behind them, the soft scuff of Keds in the dust.

"Where does this hallway go?" she whispers.

"One of the kitchens."

He's shuffling like a football player now, lolloping sideways with all the grace of a desperate crab, and Dez wishes there was enough space to squeeze around and leave him as fodder for whoever is in the passage behind them, but there's no room, and that's the problem. Finally he elbows another panel open and bursts out of the narrow tunnel. Dez is grateful for the light, the fresh air — until she sees what's waiting for them.

It's an industrial kitchen, the sort of place you don't show guests, where the real work gets done — like something from *Top Chef*, big enough to allow a dozen people to cook at once. Yet more servants are arrayed in a big circle around a long butcherblock counter. Not the pretty, shiny, oiled kind in design magazines — this is a utilitarian medieval behemoth used for the messy part of cooking, the chopping and butchering. Bill and Marie huddle on the other side of the counter. Two pink-clad servants stand behind them, and Dez wonders what sharply pointed instruments are digging into their well-bred spines.

"You put me down right now!" a familiar voice barks, and Uncle James is dragged into the room by two men in pink.

It's funny — in the movies, he always seems like the tallest, strongest, most handsome man around, but in person, he's probably six feet tall and almost average. Before today, Dez would've believed that he could fly a jet, rappel off the side of a mountain, tame a wild horse, romance a twenty-year-old. His charisma is off the charts, like he signed a deal with the devil for immortal charm and impossibly good luck. But now he looks every one of his years, struggling in the clutches of two much younger men in pink uniforms.

"Pardon me."

A hand pushes Dez's shoulder, and Valerie walks between her and Patrick as if she's merely passing by on a subway platform. The knife in her hand is freshly bloodied, and Dez shivers to think she was behind them in the passage mere moments ago.

What's odd, she realizes, is that no one has taken the hoe from her or the pitchfork from Patrick, nor have she and Patrick attempted to use their weapons. It's like they're caught in some kind of strange pantomime, some theater show where they've forgotten their lines but are still quite sure they belong on stage.

The two men in pink have dragged James to the counter, where a third man grabs his feet so they can muscle him onto his back on the scarred wood.

"What do you want?" he barks, and Dez hears shades of an army captain he played once in a blockbuster movie.

"For you to lie down and try to relax," Valerie says, brushing his hair back from his forehead and revealing a line of hair plugs. "Like you always told us: darling, this won't hurt a bit."

16

Someone hands Valerie a set of restraints — they look old and worn, not newly bought — and James tries to fight her as she gets one around his wrist and runs it under the counter to his other wrist. He's writhing up off the wood, kicking his feet, but he's not as strong as he used to be, likely never was as strong as he seemed in the movies. Two of the women wrap nylon ropes around his ankles and tie them to the counter's legs, and then *People*'s Sexiest Man of the Year 2006 is lying on his back like a bug, spread-eagled on a counter, shouting that he wants to see a lawyer.

One of the pink-clad women steps up behind him and sticks something in his open, screaming mouth — a stick wrapped in leather? She holds it there by either end, like she's force-feeding him corn on the cob. And as he has no choice but to go silent, his eyes go round with understanding — and terror.

"Everyone knows that James likes the ladies," Valerie says, running a finger over the crow's feet that women still find so appealing and making him flinch away. "But the paparazzi always assume that the women also like James. Maybe the ones that have a choice do. Maybe the ones in Hollywood do. We've seen the magazines, the string of gorgeous starlets. Limos, flowers, the best table at Nobu. You treat them so well, James. And when you leave them with a souvenir, you pay for that, too. You have a doctor on retainer. I bet his office is clean and white and full of sunlight. Probably smells like lavender."

One of the women brings over a tray covered in surgical instruments, the sort of thing Dez sees in her nightmares. Scalpels, scissors, needles, clamps, things she can't name or describe that can only exist to pull flesh apart or pin it back together. Her body takes a step back, but a gentle hand between her shoulder blades stops her, holds her in place.

There are servants behind her, like the servants behind Bill and Marie. There is no retreat.

She is meant to be a spectator, a voyeur.

This — whatever this is. She has to watch it.

They *want* her to watch it.

Valerie picks up a scalpel, holds it up in the cold fluorescent light as if considering it for the first time.

"But here on the Island, we didn't get limos or flowers. There is no clean, white doctor's office. Some of us were barely women. What happened to us happened in the servants' quarters, strapped down with these very restraints. Your genes weren't the ones they wanted, the ones they demanded. Male lions kill the cubs that aren't theirs, so Grandfather had to get rid of the evidence of your many desires. Decades of children, James. Taken from us, and our sisters and cousins and mothers, God rest their souls, because you don't like the way condoms feel."

James's head thrashes back and forth, his eyes closed, his hands opening and closing fruitlessly. He was in a movie about a magician once where he escaped a cage underwater, but he can't escape this. He probably used a stunt double then, anyway.

"Raise your hand if James gave you pills or sent you to the knife," she says.

Dez sees seven hands raised.

She realizes in that moment that there are no servants over forty, that besides Mr. Rose she hasn't seen one the entire time she's been here.

If they get rid of the unwanted children… what do they do with the adults who can no longer work? Or to the women who are no longer beautiful and pliable?

God rest their souls, Valerie said.

A chill sweeps down Dez's neck, a shiver of pure terror as realization dawns.

She still recalls the NDA firmly stating that the servants here are loyal and well compensated. She now knows that both those things are lies. The NDA also called them a family. She's beginning to see how that is horrifyingly true.

"Abigail had it the worst." Valerie holds out the scalpel. A young woman in pink—so beautiful, with golden skin and sky-blue eyes and cornsilk hair, she could be a movie star — steps forward and delicately holds the blade. She could be Patrick's sister.

Jesus, maybe she is.

If all the Ruskin men take what they want from the female servants, like James apparently has…

Dez looks around.

It's a sea of blond and light brown hair, eyes ranging from blue to gray.

No wonder all the women look alike.

No wonder *all of them* look alike.

No wonder there aren't any children running around.

That she can see.

Abigail steps up to James and looks down at him, her eyes simmering with transcendently beautiful rage. "I wasn't allowed to speak, or you hit me," she says softly. "But you liked it when I fought you. You told me to whimper. I had bruises on my thighs, teeth marks on my shoulders."

She delicately places the scalpel between her teeth as she reaches out to unbutton his snowy white shirt, revealing a white undershirt.

"You were never sweet or kind, not like in your movies. You saw me as a thing to conquer. Not even a person. That's what you do." She looks up at Bill, then Patrick. "All of you. You're taught that we're things, so you can treat us like things."

She pulls the white undershirt out of the tuxedo pants, revealing the softness of an aging man's belly, the garish orange-brown of a fake tan, artfully shaded with fake abs. He's still in reasonable shape, but definitely not like in the movies. A trail of golden hair curls merrily down the center of his torso and disappears into the black trousers. Abigail takes the scalpel out of her mouth, holds it over his exposed stomach.

"The doctor had to scrape the last one out of me. It was infected. I had a fever. I almost died. You... you filled me with pain." The shining blade touches the skin, but her mouth is a thin line. She can't quite bring herself to do it. Then she takes a deep, shuddering breath.

"Let's see what we can scrape out of you."

The scalpel draws a line of red across the artificially tanned skin. James bucks and writhes, his screams muffled by the leather-wrapped wood another woman is holding in his mouth, pulling it back at the corners, pressing it into his flesh.

Dez has never watched a surgery before — she has no morbid curiosity in such things and vastly prefers cutting cloth to slicing into a steak. She doesn't want to see what lies beneath that surface, but when she tries to turn away, firm hands turn her back.

The scalpel is deeper now, digging in, blood running down the sides of James's stomach, painting the edges of his clean white shirt, pooling underneath him.

"Agnes. Muriel. Tiffany," Valerie calls.

At her urging, three more women step forward. The woman with the tray of instruments holds it out, and they each select something sharp. One woman has — well, they looked like scissors, but now Dez thinks they must be a sort of tweezers. Forceps? She's pulling back a corner of skin like the peel of a stubborn apple. Another woman pries apart the cut Abigail has made with a pair of tongs, viciously turning a simple line into a gaping chasm. It fills with blood as his body rises off the counter, back arched as another woman reaches within and uses her forceps to pull out —

God.

Oh, God.

A long, pink piece of intestine, almost like a sausage.

She keeps pulling.

The women poke and prod, cut and pull, digging around like children playing in a sandbox, curious to see what will happen next.

The sounds James is making are unearthly, horrid, the mewlings of a dying thing.

Another woman appears, selects a scalpel, and goes to stand near his head. She slices into the corners of his mouth, pulled taut by the wrapped stick, a swift flick on each side.

"You always told us we were prettier when we smiled," she says.

And then Abigail frowns, considers her scalpel, and stabs it into James's chest, in a pectoral muscle, maybe. Red runs down his ribs as she withdraws it. The action was almost experimental, and when she stabs him again, it's with more conviction. Soon multiple women are stabbing him, scalpels and kitchen knives flashing up and down, red flecking the neat pink uniforms. No one says a word. The only sounds come from James's incoherent screaming around the leather-wrapped stick and the soft punch of metal in flesh. Dez closes her eyes, but it doesn't help. She can still hear it, so her brain supplies the images. It felt like hours, but it has been perhaps three minutes, tops, since the first blade entered unmarred flesh.

Finally, James goes quiet, and Dez looks again. Someone has slit his throat — no way to know who. He's surrounded by women holding blood-tipped instruments. As soon as James's body goes limp, they step back. There's blood everywhere, the sound of dripping, loops of intestine spilling out, a terrible, earthy, septic smell. He looks like a high school dissection gone wrong, not at all like the man smiling from the movie posters.

The silence is too loud. Bill and Marie are holding each other, Patrick is frozen, the servants are waiting for something, and Dez can't handle this strange, still moment.

"What happened to the doctor?" she asks. Her voice is a rough whisper, as if all the screaming has found a home inside of her.

Valerie turns to look at her.

"We killed him because he disagreed with our plan. He was going to tell them. We threw him in the ocean, after. Like Mr. Rose, he was an outsider. He had a choice."

Their eyes meet, and Dez sees a steely will there, someone with no options pushed to a place of desperation. There's a recognition between them.

Valerie wants her to say something, but Dez doesn't know what to say. She has never smelled the inside of a human body before. It reminds her of pennies dropped in salt water full of shit. The dripping won't stop. She never dreamed a person could be so full of blood.

Something moves in the corner of her vision, and Patrick's pitchfork slams into Valerie, knocking her sideways. There's a stupid desperation to his movements; he's all lizard brain, no intelligence left at all. He's not even using the tines as he screams his rage and raises the pitchfork again. Two men grab him by the arms and pull him back as the other women help Valerie to stand. Blood coats her palms from where she fell on the floor, her apron knocked askew. Another man yanks the pitchfork from Patrick's hand, and he screams over and over again with the aggressive, useless lunacy of a tired toddler having a breakdown. He sounds just like the boys at the pool.

There's a scuffle across the kitchen as Bill and Marie use their son's distraction to bolt from the room, breaking past the loose circle of servants. No one stops them. A woman rubs her shoulder where Marie bumped her on her way out and mutters, "Bitch."

No one reaches for Dez. They're not even hurting Patrick. Just restraining him.

"You done?" Valerie asks.

Patrick spits, a sad, dry little glob landing on her collar. "You're gonna pay for this."

Valerie reaches out and pats his cheek. "Patrick, honey, I've been paying my whole life, remember? That's just what I get for being born female. But don't worry — it's almost your turn."

She walks away, leaving bloody footprints. The rest of the servants join her, filing out the door. The women who... who killed James, they walk out together, almost giddy. When nearly everyone is gone, the two men holding Patrick release him.

"Henry, come on. You're going along with this?" he says to one of the men.

The man pushes his sunglasses up on his head to reveal blue-gray eyes. He could be Patrick's twin — almost.

"If I was half a foot taller and a bully, I'd be living your life," Henry says. "And actually doing something with it. So, yeah, I'm going along with it." He smiles, a chilling reflection of Patrick's grin. "You don't have much longer, brother."

17

Dez is stunned that the servants leave her and Patrick standing there. No restraints, no threats. Sure, they've been allowed to run away before, but this… it feels like someone putting one of those electronic collars on a dog and leaving them alone in the yard because they know there's an invisible fence.

They must know —

Oh.

"Come on," she says, grabbing Patrick's tux jacket sleeve and pulling him toward the other exit, the one the servants didn't take.

The air smells immeasurably better in the hallway, and she's never been so thankful for the scent of freshly cut flowers. Patrick must be out of it, as he's not generally the sort of person who would allow himself to be dragged bodily anywhere, especially not through his childhood home. They don't encounter a single soul as she pulls him up the grand staircase.

"Come on," she mutters, yanking his arm. "Hurry. We've got to get to your suite."

That wakes him up enough to say, "I'm not in the mood."

"I don't care."

She remembers this door, still wears the bruise from being dragged here herself. She opens the door and pulls Patrick inside, immensely grateful and somewhat resentful that here, at least, there is a lock.

"Take off your shoes."

When he doesn't take off his shoes, just stands there as stiff and stupid as Frankenstein's monster rebooting, she tries to tug off his tuxedo jacket, but he rips his arm away from her.

"Jesus, Dez. I told you. I'm not in the mood, okay? That's my *uncle* — "

"Patrick, you idiot, I'm not trying to fuck you. I'm trying to see if they put a tracker on you."

His head jerks back like she slapped him, and his eyes blink like the spinning pinwheel on a Macbook. "What?"

"They keep letting us go. Every time we see someone — every time they — " She can't say it, what they keep doing. "Afterwards, they let us go. Right? You would think they'd tie us up and make us just stay in one place and watch, but instead it's like they're herding us where they want us, then just... leaving us alone. So they're not worried about losing us. There must be a reason. I changed my entire outfit, but you — "

"Shit."

He shrugs out of his tuxedo jacket and throws it on the ground, and she runs her fingers over the seams, tugs at the tags, investigates each silken pocket. Just a few days ago, she would've given anything, anything in the world to hold a Tom Ford tuxedo, but now it reeks of fear and reminds her of watching blood pool under James's identical black trousers.

She doesn't find anything, but then again, she doesn't know what she's looking for. If rescue vets can put a microchip the size of a grain of rice in a cat's neck, who knows what tiny, expensive, futuristic device might be somewhere in Patrick's suit? It seems like the kind of tech they would have here, whether to make sure the Ruskin family was safe when traveling or to keep track of the children. Since they don't trust many outsiders, outside of Mr. Rose and the dead doctor, it's likely the servants were trained to handle all their tech.

Patrick shucks off his shoes and pants, then struggles with his bow tie. If Dez was still pretending she gave a shit, she would help him, but they're way past that now. Instead, she inspects his shoes, looking inside the rigid leather and running her fingers along the laces. His shirt is soaked in sweat, but the buttons all seem normal.

"Did you find it?" he asks, standing there stupidly in tighty whities, a white undershirt, and black socks.

"Am I triumphantly holding up a tracking chip and saying, 'Yay, I found it, the nightmare is over?' No? Then probably not."

Patrick finds it impossible to look cool and imposing in his current state of dishabille, but he tries. "You're a major bitch when shit gets real, you know that?"

Dez chucks one of his shoes at him, and he fumbles to catch it. "Yes, Patrick, when a holiday weekend with my new beau turns

146

into, into fucking *Saw for Rich People*, I certainly can be a bitch. What the fuck is wrong with your family?"

He scoffs and turns away, rummaging through an armoire twice the size of hers and putting on a pair of expensive athletic pants. "Nothing is wrong with my family. When you have this much money accrued over several generations, you have to take measures to protect your assets and privacy."

"How old were you when they forced you to memorize that sentence word for word?"

Another scoff. It does not look good on him. "They didn't force me to do anything."

"I know you didn't come up with it on your own. You're not that smart."

He takes off the undershirt and shrugs into a navy blue t-shirt. "And you're not that pretty. I'm surprised they even let you on the Island. I was sure they were going to reject you. Only invited you so you'd go down on me. There must be something special about you that I've never noticed."

Dez knows that he's baiting her, but she's not going to give him the satisfaction of begging to know what is or is not special about her. Her fashion design skills, grades, tenacity, and, yes, looks are the things she has going for her. Outside of that, she's just the poor daughter of a hotel housekeeper cut off by her also-poor family for having a red-headed bastard. But…

"So your family only lets special people on the Island?" she asks. "So everybody here is super *special*?"

His perfect nose is in the air now. "Yes. My mother is a Caulfield. Genevieve is a Canady. Christiane is a Durant. Old bloodlines. Proven bloodlines. Only the best. They wouldn't let my last girlfriend set foot here, and she was a solid ten, not a…" He looks her up and down. "Eight, if I'm being kind."

"I'm at least a nine, and you know it."

"Maybe before you started being a bitch." He puts on a pair of sneakers and runs his hands through his hair. "Let's barricade ourselves in here," he says, looking around. "If we push the bed up against the door, they can't get in."

Dez walks to the huge window and looks down. The entire island is tastefully lit, perfect spotlights ensuring that no one could possibly sneak around in the dark. The ceilings are high, and it's a steep drop to giant century plants that would probably leave them torn to shreds. There is no ledge outside, no balcony, no trellis. The tennis court is just beyond the landscaping but offers no sanctuary under its aggressive fluorescent lights. Patrick is already tugging the bed over toward the door, but it's enormous and heavy, maybe bigger than a king, and solid wood. He's exactly the kind of man who thinks he's capable of just shoving it into place and calling it a day.

His tux is still on the ground, and Dez is fairly certain she didn't miss anything when she was looking for trackers. Her eyes rove from Patrick's sneakers, up his sweatpants and tee, to the straining muscles of his arms as he pulls the bedpost with all his might. It's moved approximately two inches, judging by the marks on the carpet.

And then she notices his big gold ring — the one he always wears.

His brothers each had one, as did his uncles and grandfather.

The family crest.

If Dez wanted to track someone, it might as well be using a piece of jewelry they never, ever take off, a piece of gold of which they are annoyingly proud. The women didn't have the same crest, but she recalls their enormous diamond rings.

She opens her mouth to tell Patrick to take it off and then... Doesn't.

If she's right, they can track him, but they can't track her.

There are benefits to this situation.

"You work on that. I'm going to get some food and water," she says. "From the other kitchen."

He looks at her like she's insane. "You're hungry right now?"

"More thirsty. They turned off the water. It's been hours. We have to keep our strength up if we want to get off the Island. And honestly, even if you barricade us in, as it is, they can just wait until we die of dehydration in three days."

His eyes, as ever, seem to weigh her. He shrugs. "Do what you want, I guess. Not like you'd be much help moving the bed. I'll try to leave it open enough for you to squeeze through." And then, almost as an afterthought and in no way sincere, "Be careful."

She nods at him and slips out of his suite, this palatial chamber of utmost comforts where she'd expected to spend much of her weekend at his sexual beck and call. This — God, it's practically an apartment — is an absolute dream, even nicer than her own room, with a full sitting area, electric fireplace, dining table, and an enormous bathroom. There is no sign of Patrick in it, not like a guy's bedroom back home with his old trophies and skateboards and posters plastered on the wall. It might as well be a hotel room, and she wonders what it must've been like, growing up in a place where you were simply a Ruskin and not, in particular, yourself.

The hallway is silent, the grand stairwell empty. She scouts from overhead, notes that the blood she saw earlier in the foyer is drying. The front doors are open, letting in a jasmine-scented night breeze. It feels too exposed. Dez scurries back down the hallway, past her own room, down the secret stairs, and to the kitchen. Relief floods her when she sees that it's empty. She throws open one of two enormous fridges, but immediately slams the doors shut when she finds Grandmother's head sitting on a silver platter.

Outside of... that... the fridge is empty.

She tries the other fridge, and it's empty, too. She wonders if the servants threw everything into the sea or perhaps moved it to their own quarters. Every shelf is sparkling clean. When she pushes the button that should produce water, nothing comes out. She swallows, hating how dry her throat is, and starts opening cabinets, searching for a glass. The first thing she finds is a teacup, and when she holds it under the tap, nothing comes out.

"Shit."

She'd at least hoped for one last, sad spurt. She ends up scooping water out of the back of the powder room toilet, tasting a vague twinkle of bleach and lemon but knowing she needs the water if she wants to stay alive, much less alert. She hasn't eaten since they brought her that ostentatious tray of sandwiches for lunch, and the leftovers were cleared long ago. She's very aware that if she wasn't in absolute shock and fighting for her life, she'd be hungry to the point of nausea.

Outside, a sound system scrapes to life with a tooth-grinding screech.

"Marie! Will! Patrick! Whoever's still here — "

It's Bill Ruskin, and he doesn't sound like he's calling out because he wants to.

"Please. Come help me. I'm at the tennis courts. They're going to — "

The sound system cuts off.

There's no way Dez is going to the tennis courts, but she definitely wants to see what's happening out there. She runs back upstairs and considers the line of doors before going into the biggest pair of double doors among the suites. If Patrick's rooms are elegant, this place is opulent, splendid, glamorous — clearly reserved for the most powerful of the Ruskins.

Dez knows she's right when she spots Marie at the window, looking down, half-hidden by the heavy white curtains. Nearly everything else in the estate is done in shades of pink, but this room is all white, as bright and clean as a hotel lobby. And why not? Not all roses are pink, after all.

Marie's eyes flick to her coldly before returning to the scene outside. Dez takes her place at the opposite side of the windows from her once idol, likewise concealing herself behind the curtains. Marie doesn't challenge this move, and Dez no longer cares what the woman thinks about her, anyway. Not that she can stop staring.

"Marie, please!" Bill wails, and Marie closes her eyes, but not for long.

Outside, the tennis court stands out from the rest of the Island, a flaming shade of terra-cotta among all the whites and greens and pinks of the gardens. It's surrounded by a low white fence, as if the Ruskins are so confident that they'll never hit a ball out of bounds that it doesn't need to be more than knee-high.

Or maybe they just know there are dozens of people who have no choice but to go chase any wayward serves.

Bill is standing in the center of the court, tied to the net at his wrists and ankles, utterly ridiculous in his black tuxedo pants and nothing else. His body is still very fit for his age, naturally tanned and looking remarkably like Patrick's. His ring winks in the glare of the lights overhead, and Dez looks over and notices that Marie doesn't seem to have the same Ruskin ring — and that she's removed her wedding rings. Maybe she's come to the same conclusions Dez has about the wisdom of sticking with her man just now.

Two men in pink roll a machine out across the clay court, a blocky thing that Dez can't identify. A long black wire trails behind it, connected to an extension cord. Dez is not surprised when Valerie approaches and stands beside the machine. She's wearing a headset microphone, the kind stage actors use.

"Marie, Patrick, Desirée. I know you're all out there. Won't someone come save poor Bill? Are you going to make him face this alone?"

Marie exhales in annoyance but does not move from her post. Patrick does not suddenly appear outside. Dez is well aware that Valerie did not mention Christiane or Genevieve.

"Looks like it's just us, Bill," Valerie says. She steps up, puts a hand on his cheek, which makes him flinch away. "Or, should I say… Dad."

18

The word echoes in the night air.

Dad. Dad. Dad.

Valerie looks up at Marie, whose eyes are glued to the tableau outside. She doesn't smile or frown or flinch or cry or look away.

She knows.

She has always known.

"Oh, I'm sorry, Ruskins don't have daughters, do they?" Valerie continues. "Ruskins have perfect sons and imperfect servants. That's how it's always been. No birth certificates for the girls, no travel documents. No last names. If you're a girl, you always know your place. If you're a boy, you have until kindergarten to prove you're going to be the best. Isn't that right? Just like *horses*."

"I never had a choice," Bill says weakly, barely a whisper through Valerie's microphone.

"You didn't have a choice? You? Now one of the ten richest men in the world? Don't lie to me. You've lied enough."

Through the mic, Dez can hear Bill's voice, hear various

apologies and promises. He even begs a little, she thinks. But Valerie is the one with full control of the microphone, and she's not done.

"I wasn't sure how to kill you. It's a big deal, killing your secret father, you know? I always assumed it was you. And then, when I was fifteen, you called me to your personal suite. Did that not sicken you? I'm either your daughter or your niece or your half-sister. How could you do that?"

More mumbling.

"It's not like that," Dez hears Bill say.

Valerie slaps him, a sharp *crack*.

"You don't get to say what it's like anymore. Your time is up. We heard about that, you know? The Me Too movement, Time's Up. You spent so much energy making sure we couldn't get online, but guess who watches the cameras? Guess who confiscates the guest phones? Guess who tidies up the tablets your latest golden children leave by the pool? We're the ones who troubleshoot your secret connections, asshole. We're smarter than you think. We're all Ruskins, after all, one way or the other."

Bill's voice is unintelligible but faster now, and Dez can imagine the promises and threats he must be panic-vomiting at this girl who holds complete power over his life and death.

But hearing this — understanding what's been happening on this island for generations — Dez no longer has any pity for anyone wearing that Ruskin ring.

This family has been breeding people like their precious polo ponies, choosing their bloodlines, selecting only the strongest, tallest offspring to support, and using the rest in the silent part of the family business. Housekeepers and maids and cooks and security and pool boys and…

Those poor women. Those poor little girls.

Those poor boys in Anthony's attic bower.

They never had a chance.

They should've had everything.

There was more than enough for them all.

As Valerie steps back, Dez realizes whose side she's on.

"So we all talked about it, and we remembered how much we hated you on the tennis court. Forcing us to play, angrily hitting balls to make us chase them like dogs. Losing makes you mean and winning makes you cruel. Half the time one of us ends up bent over that net. So now it's your turn to see what it feels like to be on the other end of a killer serve."

Valerie stands behind the blocky contraption, and Dez understands now. It's a tennis ball machine.

As if reading her mind, Valerie says, "You told me once this was the most powerful machine money can buy. Let's see what it does real close up."

Dez barely hears the machine launch the first ball, but she hears Bill's grunt of pain and sees an immediate welt rise, almost burgundy, on his belly. Valerie hooks the microphone over Bill's head delicately before taking up her post behind the machine again. The next ball lands, and Bill doubles over with a moan of pain. There's another welt on his chest.

Pop.

Pop.

Pop.

And then Valerie does something that sends the machine into overtime. A ball shoots out every few seconds, slamming into Bill Ruskin's torso. He bucks and flails like people in movies being shot with machine guns. Everywhere a ball hits, a red welt rises, welt upon welt. One breaks the skin, almost like a rug burn. The machine doesn't stop, and Valerie concentrates the hits in just one place, more blood blooming as the soft skin of an old man's tummy gives way. Bill moans and groans and then starts screaming the word, "Stop!" over and over again.

Pop.

Pop.

Pop.

"They're going to rupture his liver," Marie says to the room as if Dez isn't there, as if she's watching her husband undergo a surgery that isn't being performed to her standards.

Valerie takes back the microphone and holds it up to her lips.

"This is taking too long. Bring out the croquet mallets."

The machine doesn't stop pummeling Bill, and Bill doesn't stop screaming, but four women in pink arrive, carrying the croquet mallets Dez noticed outside yesterday, all white with dainty pastel stripes. They hold the mallets like they know how to use them — like they've been waiting all their lives to really put them to the test.

Valerie turns off the ball machine, and Dez exhales in relief now that the repetitive popping sound is finally over. Bill's cries subside to soft sobs.

"When no one from the family was on the Island and we were very young, we played croquet," Valerie says softly, taking back the mic and hooking it over her ears. "We never had pretty dresses and Easter bonnets, because there were no fancy Ruskin daughters, but we would dress up in what we found in the attic. Old, discarded things. Ragged minks and moth-eaten hats. And we would pretend that we were you. That we were real Ruskins just like you."

She holds out her hand, and one of the women gives her a croquet mallet. She holds it properly, prissily, and pretends to take a shot, as if shooting a ball through its hoops along the lawn, then scoops the mallet up onto her shoulder like a baseball bat.

"We *are* you, but we had to pretend. Just to savor a sliver of what you enjoy every day." A pause. "Put your head up, Dad. At least look at me."

Bill's body heaves as his head fights his neck. He looks like a boxer who's gone twelve rounds but won't quite give up. As soon as his head is up, his eyes perhaps focusing on the young woman before him, Valerie rears back and slams the croquet mallet into the side of his head.

Crack.

His head bounces to the other side and swings back down, and Valerie gives her mallet back to the other woman. After a brief pause, she bashes Bill's bare toes, leaving a bloody mush on the clay court. The four women take turns gleefully whacking whatever hasn't yet been destroyed. Another head shot sends teeth and blood flying. Bill's other foot soon matches the first, not flattened like a cartoon character but crushed and mushy. Dez can't look away when one of the women slams the mallet into his crotch. If he deserves nothing else — which he does — he deserves that one especially.

What Dez is watching — it's very *Clockwork Orange*. A bit of the old ultraviolence. And yet this isn't random, this is purposeful. This is studied. This is retribution. There's a kind of violence that is meted out over years, over generations, a polite and civilized violence made of rules and psychological warfare and catastrophic power imbalances, a quiet violence that arrives in the night with a gently closed door and a manicured finger to soft lips. That violence is death by a thousand cuts, something almost endurable, no less vicious but a lot less bloody. And then there is a kind of violence that is undeniable, sudden, animalistic, authentic, and final.

Dez is seeing the latter in person for the first time, and she begins to understand why someone invented Molotov cocktails. There's a strange, deep glee, somewhere inside her, a spark hungry for tinder to burn. So many men have reached to touch her against her will, and she had to take it, had to accept a professor's hand on the small of her back, an old man's hug that goes on just a little too long, her mom's manager fingering the hem of her dress at Thanksgiving and telling her she looks so grown up. She has silently longed to bite their fingers off and spit them back. Watching someone else take that privilege, watching the servants exact their revenge...

Dez doesn't hate it.

She just wishes her name wasn't one of the three Valerie just called.

Down on the court, the only noise is the jolly, bouncing thud of wood hitting flesh and bone. Finally, the girls step back, satisfied with their grisly work. Bill Ruskin hangs like a dime-store Jesus from the tennis net, arms out wide, on his knees in a puddle of blood. Dez can't tell if he's still alive. It doesn't really matter. There's no way he'll live through this. No way he deserves to.

Valerie turns to face the house, points directly at Patrick's room.

"You're next, bro," she says.

19

In the silence that follows, Marie Caulfield-Ruskin has the temerity to look at her watch.

"What, did you reserve the court next?" Dez asks.

The look Marie gives her is withering. "No. I'm counting down until the Coast Guard's nightly rounds. They circle the Island at midnight every night. Once the servants are done with their little game and off the court, I'm going to spell out HELP on these windows. If you'd like to live through this, go get all your lipsticks and help me. I noticed you were wearing Chanel's Gabrielle last night."

"Oh, so you noticed me?"

Marie's signature smirk. "Oh, yes, Desirée. I know more about you than you think. Maybe more than you know about yourself." She tilts her head toward the double doors. "Lipstick. Now. I want you to write an H and an E in the windows of the suite just on the other side of this one. The E will need to be backwards for obvious reasons."

When Dez doesn't immediately do her bidding, she adds, "Move!"

Dez looks back down to the tennis court and finds the servants missing. Bill is lolling forward, the net bowed behind him. Blood drips from his mouth — what's left of it. His face looks like the oatmeal Dez's mom used to make for her with the fresh raspberries she snatched from the hotel's breakfast buffet.

"I'm not doing it because you told me to, or because I buy into any of this classist bullshit," she says, heading for the door. "I'm doing it because it's smart."

When Marie nods in approval and says, "Good girl," Dez wants to throw up.

Her room is untouched, and she grabs the two red lipsticks she brought. Even now, even here, she hates wasting them; they were a splurge, and she treats them like gold. On her way back, she notices that Patrick's door is open and wonders where he's gone to hide on his own, now that the servants have claimed him as their next victim.

It doesn't matter. She'd thought him silly, rude, and assumptive but relatively harmless in the way of all man-boys playing their frivolous games until it's time to grow up and run the company. But now she's realizing that no one could be raised this way without becoming some sort of sociopath. She knows Patrick has committed sins worthy of punishment, or else he wouldn't be so frightened of getting his just desserts. If he was without fault, he wouldn't have to run.

He'd be on their side.

Instead, he is their prey.

The next suite is the one where Dez has been told to write letters in the windows. When she opens the unlocked door, she immediately understands that this room belonged to Anthony and Christiane. She knows this because Christiane is lying on the bed, very dead, her pregnant belly sliced open and deflated, blood soaking the melon-pink comforter. There is a bullet hole in her forehead, suggesting that at least her ending was quick — and that she was gone before they claimed the baby.

Dez didn't think Christiane would survive the night, but she is surprised at the utter devastation that echoes in her body to see what was taken from her so easily. Yes, this woman married a rapist, and if the NDA to get on the Island was that severe, the one to marry into the family must be even more explicit and secure. This woman knew what was happening here and signed her name multiple times to agree that she would keep this secret, be part of it. Patrick said she was — a Durant or a Canady? Another one of the ten richest families in the country, their legacies built on the backs of slavery, colonization, pollution, manufactured drug epidemics. She was complicit. And now she is gone.

This does not bode well for Dez.

When she signed the NDA, she didn't know about… all this. But she came here for selfish reasons, hoping to use Patrick as a springboard to her own desires.

Still, she knows in her bones that the moment she discovered one instance of the rapists-all-the-way-down situation on the Island, she would've feigned appendicitis to get the hell out forever.

Dez read an article for a psychology class once about loss aversion, about how the pain of having something taken away is twice as powerful as the pleasure of gaining something, how losing money is especially painful for people who are accustomed to it. She's never had money, so she cannot relate. These people — these rich people — wanted to uphold their way of life more than anything, no matter who it hurt. Maybe Christiane didn't deserve this… but she probably did.

Dez pulls the pink chenille blanket off the back of the couch and lays it gently over what's left of Christiane. She briefly thinks about writing on the windows in the congealing blood, then shakes her head.

It's getting to her.

Now that she has a moment of quiet, a moment in which no one is dying in front of her, no weapon is pointed at her, there is a razor-sharp glimmer of reality through the gloriously blurry haze of adrenaline.

This is happening.

It is really happening.

All this death, all this blood, all this rage —

It is not some elaborate play, a cleverly designed escape room, a staged spectacle designed to surprise and titillate the tragically sated.

It is real, and it could be the end of her, even though she has more in common with the servants than she does with their victims.

The people with the weapons don't know her, don't know that she's not one of… *them*.

The Ruskins, and people like them.

And there is no way for Dez to deliver this message that won't sound like the lying, squealing, mealy-mouthed pleas of a desperate man watching his bloodied intestines pile in sausage loops on his Gucci loafers.

No, words can't fix this. Dez has been scraped down to her core, whittled away to the wild animal that once hid under borrowed Versace.

The sky outside is dark, the Island lit garishly below. Dez doesn't know what time it is, has forgotten the day. She is prey now, and prey can only live in the moment. Her only thought is escape.

She can imagine a boat's light swinging around, a boring routine, the same way it does every night, and revealing two windows dripping with blood beside two windows in neat lipstick. Marie will probably use a font with a serif. Something classy.

But no. Blood will run.

And Dez does not want to touch Christiane's blood.

She unscrews her least favorite of the two lipsticks and starts her H on the far-right window. It's harder than it seems to make a line thick enough to be visible, and she feels like a child scribbling with the cheap kind of crayon, the ones that are too waxy and always drew a sharp delineation between the kids with money and the kids who did their school shopping at the dollar store. She desperately wanted the Crayola box with the sharpener, but her mom could never afford it. It's a strange thought to have now, but… she resents it. Someone who grew up too poor to buy ninety-six crayons is not meant to die in thrifted Lululemons on this island.

She's halfway through the backwards E when the door to the room opens.

"Are the letters thick enough?" she asks.

"It won't matter."

That voice is not Marie.

It's Valerie.

Dez spins, recognizing her mistake. She's left her hoe out of reach, its concrete bludgeon useless. All she has right now are two tubes of lipstick, and there's nothing nearby, no makeshift weapons, not even a lamp. She doesn't even have her electric candle. Eyes locked on Valerie, her hand goes to a nearby piece of art on the wall, a dainty framed watercolor, but... it doesn't budge.

"Glued down," Valerie confirms. "The Ruskins trust no one. Not even each other."

Dez slams a fist into the glass, but it's just plastic.

The look Valerie gives her is amused and pitying.

"I'm not here to kill you, Desirée."

"Okay..."

"Let me go!" Marie screeches from the hall. "Don't you dare!"

"You need to be there." Valerie wipes at her cheek, where a constellation of blood drops has dried. "You need to know about Patrick."

"I know he's a piece of shit."

Valerie chuckles. "Come on, then. If you walk, we don't have to drag you."

Dez can see the outline of the gun in Valerie's pocket, how it weighs down her apron. All these deaths, and for the most part, the gun has been unnecessary.

"How are you tracking us?"

"The rings. And cameras."

Dez nods. She's glad she was right, but it's small comfort.

She puts the cap on her lipstick, sets both tubes on the table, and takes one last look at the lump on the bed.

"She knew about Anthony," Valerie confirms. "What he did to those guys. Then, and now. And that baby? Came from a twisted three-way with Will and Patrick, so they don't know whose it is. Not that they care, as long as it's one of them."

"Where's the baby?"

Valerie gestures for her to go first. "Somewhere safe, where she'll be loved like she deserves."

In the hall, two men hold Marie by the upper arms. Her wrists are bound together with a long string of pearls — her trademark necklace put to a new use. Most pearls look alike to all but the most discriminating connoisseur, but Dez would know Marie's pearls anywhere. They're a warm, golden white, with silk knots between each pearl, strong enough to last centuries. Dez can't help wondering if this is how the original owner of those pearls looked when she was led to the guillotine for similar crimes — was she haughty, angry, unable to comprehend the change in her fortunes? This Marie looks like she wants to bite every single one of her captors, wants to sink her ice-white veneers in down to the bone. When Valerie motions Dez forward, she walks. She does not wish to be bound, by pearls or otherwise.

The servants lead her around the corner and past her own door. A man in pink gestures her into an open room, the Belle de Londres room. This one was designed for children, done in soft pink and light green and cream with a rocking horse, a small table and chairs, and a train set in colors that match the room instead of a child's attention span.

Patrick sits on one of the two twin beds, his face red and his usually careful hair an absolute wreck. Instead of pearls, he's simply zip-tied. Stretching between the beds, where a bedside table might go, is a large blanket chest, maybe six feet long. The paint is new, but the corners seem worn, the wood solid in a way furniture simply isn't, anymore.

Valerie walks past Dez, briefly puts a hand on her shoulder before Marie is brought to stand beside her, their shoulders touching. Dez can smell her perfume and assumes it's custom — because she's Marie Caulfield-Ruskin, a beast of her own design. Roses are there, but not just roses. The power play of musk, a lightning burst of ozone, a dribble of rich red blood, the haughty stroke of leather. It smells like wealth now tainted with an undercurrent of unwelcome animal fear.

The room is full of servants now, and Valerie stands before Patrick.

"I think we'd all agree that Patrick is the least problematic of the current crop of Ruskin boys," she says, mussing his hair and making him flinch away. "But that doesn't mean he is without fault — "

"Val, come on. Don't do this — "

A light slap on his cheek. "Being the least problematic is not praise, golden boy. You benefit from the system. Just because you've never raped anyone — that we know of — doesn't mean you're free from sin. You knew what was happening and never stopped it. Never told anyone. Never offered any comfort. You took what you thought was yours. Every man here could've been where you are, but you took that place with pride."

"What do you want me to do? Be like Luke? Ruin Thanksgiving and then run off?"

It's as if the air leaves the room.

"Luke didn't run off, you idiot," Valerie tells him. "They got him drunk and threw him in the ocean with a cement block tied to his penny loafers. For the sharks. You can't just run off from..." She gestures at the absurd opulence of the furnishings. "All this. Not if you know the truth."

Patrick looks at Marie. "Is that true? Was Luke — "

"I don't know what happened," Marie says stiffly. "They don't tell me. I'm just as trapped as anyone else."

"I thought Luke was still out there somewhere. I kept waiting for an email..."

He trails off.

He really is as stupid as Dez assumed.

Whoever picked him may have picked wrong.

Then again, maybe the Ruskins were breeding for height, build, beauty, charisma... and a weak will. Maybe they don't want big thinkers out in the world right now. Maybe they don't want people who might question things.

"We're getting off track." Valerie walks past Patrick and stands beside the chest, gesturing to it. "Remember this, bro?"

Patrick's eyes flick unwillingly to the chest and he blanches. "Yeah, I guess."

"You guess? You're not sure? Do you think it might've been another antique chest? You think I'm remembering it wrong? Or do you just not want to admit what you did."

"We were kids, Val! Like, eight! So young. We were playing."

She shakes her head sadly. "I've heard that so many times tonight. Men excusing bad behavior by saying they were young, or that's how they were raised, or that's just how things are. It was a joke, we were playing around. Boys will be boys." She leans over, hands on her knees, to look into his gray-blue eyes, a perfect mirror of her own. "You forced me into this chest, locked it, and took the key. And then you laughed and left. All because I beat you at hide and seek. Because you weren't just a kid anymore — you were an official Ruskin brat. Because *you could*. You weren't even punished, were you?" She slaps him again, a little harder. "Don't answer that. We all know none of you were ever punished, once you were official."

Valerie flips open the top of the chest. It's empty, which is a relief. After all she's seen today, Dez was expecting razor blades, or hydrochloric acid, or —

"Put him in," Valerie says.

20

Patrick has to weigh at least one-eighty, and since he doesn't want to go in the chest, it's just not happening. Two of the men in pink maneuver him to his feet, but then he slumps over, dead weight, and they struggle to get him upright again. A third man gets involved, but human bodies are awkward, and Patrick is strong. He struggles and flops and flails until Valerie pulls out her gun.

"Remember what happened to Mr. Rose," she reminds him. "You can go in whole, or you can go in full of holes. Either is fine with me."

Patrick goes still, but he doesn't get any closer to the chest.

Valerie aims the gun at his crotch. "You know I'll do it."

"Mom, you've got to stop them," Patrick says, looking to Marie.

She holds up her pearl-wrapped wrists. "Tell me how and I will."

Patrick next glances at Dez, but he either knows she has no loyalty to him or believes her to be utterly helpless. He doesn't ask her for anything; his eyes pass right over her. He's looking for help, for understanding, for an ally, and he finds no one. After all he's seen tonight, Dez can't believe he would even try.

Reluctantly, he steps into the box until he's standing in it, bound hands stupidly out in front of him. "Okay, Val. You win. I'm in the box."

She rolls her eyes. "Get all the way in. You know that's not what I meant. Just get it over with. Now is not a great time to be petulant." The gun flops in her hand as she talks, always pointed at a different part of him.

Glaring hatred, Patrick sits, rocking back as his butt lands because his hands are bound together. Valerie walks over, puts a hand on his head, and shoves him down until he's scrunched in the box, knees bent and head tucked to his chest. He just barely fits, and it can't be comfortable.

"Go on and lock me in," he says tiredly, sounding like a spoiled child.

Valerie stands over him, staring down, smiling.

"Did you really think it would be that easy? Just… locking you in a chest until you apologize? Come on, bro. You know what we're doing here isn't a lesson. It's an extinction. This side of the family has to die so the other line can truly live. Just because you deserve it slightly less than the rest of them doesn't mean that you get to live through it." A dark pause. "Or enjoy it."

A man in pink enters the room holding a medicine ball — and a heavy one, judging by the way he's carrying it. He walks over to the chest and drops it on Patrick. Not hard enough to do real damage, but hard enough to make a point. Patrick grunts stoically but doesn't say anything.

"When you locked me in the trunk and left me in here alone, it felt like there was an elephant sitting on my chest," Valerie says as another man brings in another medicine ball and drops it on Patrick's feet with a meaty crunch that makes him gasp. "I couldn't breathe. I couldn't swallow. I had my first panic attack. I thought I was dying."

Another medicine ball arrives, then another. Almost all the room in the chest is taken up now.

"We've all had panic attacks," Patrick says, his voice rough with pain. "Are you done now?"

"No."

The next man brings in a bag of sand and upends it over Patrick in a cloud of tan powder. Patrick coughs and gags but can't get his bound hands to his face because they're trapped under a medicine ball. More and more bags of sand arrive, and Dez steps closer to see what's happening in the chest. No one stops her. The sand is all around Patrick, and he's squirming but can't move. He's trying so hard to maintain his composure, his stupidly brazen nonchalance, but he's beginning to fail, blinking against the glassy grains in his eyes and shaking his head to get away from the beige clouds.

Once the sand is covering everything except Patrick's shoulders and face, Valerie motions to a woman, who brings her a cardboard box, maybe twice the size of a shoe box. When Valerie opens it, her smile suggests she's been waiting for this moment for a long, long time.

"What you didn't know when you locked me in the chest, Patrick, was that I wasn't completely alone. A spider had laid an egg sack in there, and all my thrashing around ruptured it. They were in my clothes. My hair. My mouth."

"That's not my fault!" Patrick yelps. "We were just kids playing a game! I didn't mean anything — "

"It's not about what you mean!" she screams, her face red and the box shaking in her hands. "Actions have consequences! Just never for you — not until now."

She walks over and upends the box. To Dez's horror, hundreds of giant roaches fall out and skitter all over Patrick. Valerie slams the chest's lid down and sits on it — but, of course, Patrick can't lift the lid. His hands are under a medicine ball, covered in sand. All he can do is scream.

So he does. He screams and begs and cries, and at one point gags and spits like there is something big and crunchy in his mouth and then screams some more. Dez looks at Marie, still standing upright with her hands bound by pearls. She looks ragged, her makeup streaked with tears, her wrinkles showing, for once. Her trademark platinum bob has all the panache of a roadkill possum, and sweat stains the armpits of her gown. Dez wonders if she's crying for her husband and sons... or for herself, knowing that they will never let her go for birthing, or at least raising and supporting, these monstrous men.

Patrick finally quiets down inside the chest, and Dez wonders if they'll leave him like this or if they have more in mind.

"Who's got him?" Valerie asks.

A woman in pink steps up with a plastic terrarium held carefully by the sides.

Valerie holds it up, chuckling at what she sees within. "You know, Raymond spends a lot of time waiting at the dock. His entire job is to park the yacht and wait to ferry you assholes across to the Island. You're almost always late. And you never apologize for making anyone wait. But it's boring, just sitting on the yacht, so sometimes he goes for little hikes. Not too far, though; we know the consequences, when our trackers leave your established boundaries. And one day, he found this beautiful little specimen."

She places the terrarium on the chest and carefully loosens the lid. Dez still can't see inside, but she can guess what's within. The national park where they left the car is a wild place, and there were signs about the local flora and fauna that might be dangerous.

"Ray?"

A man in pink steps up and pulls open the top of the chest. Hundreds of roaches skitter into whatever hiding places they can to avoid the light; a few climb down the shining white sides of the chest and disappear underneath it. Dez shudders as they crawl over Patrick's face, wiggle under his hair.

"Val, Ray, please. Come on. This is enough. I've been punished, okay? I'm sorry. I'm sorry I was an asshole kid. I'm who they taught me to be. You don't know what it's like, when they take you off the Island. You have to sign things, learn new rules — "

"We were eight, Pat. It was three years after you left. You only did it because you knew you couldn't get in trouble for it anymore. You thought it was funny. You loved it — that little taste of power." Still looking him in the eyes, she gently upends the terrarium into the chest. A small brown snake flops onto the sand and immediately rattles its little tail.

"Val, no, come on. That's — that's poisonous."

"Venomous," Dez corrects without really thinking about it.

"Venomous," Valerie agrees. "But if you hold very, very still and don't make a sound, maybe he won't bite you. And, hey. At least you're not alone." With that, she slams the lid back down again and puts a shiny new lock through the hasp, clicking it shut.

"How long will you leave him in there?" Marie asks, carefully keeping her voice even.

"I already threw away the combination to the lock. So forever, I guess."

Valerie tosses the empty terrarium on the ground and dusts off her hands.

"Almost done. Shall we get on with it?"

She curtseys to Marie and walks out the door smiling. Two men tow Marie along in her wake. The rest of the servants follow. No one pushes or pulls Dez; it's as if she's been forgotten. Curious now, and well aware that there is no escape, that there is no place she can hide where they won't find her, she follows.

As she leaves the room, Patrick begins screaming for real.

21

There's nothing Dez can do for Patrick now, even if she thought he deserved help. She can't open the lock, and the box is solid wood. She knows perfectly well that the servants have taken or hidden anything that might pass for a weapon, which means she's not going to find a convenient axe or pry bar somewhere. Her concrete-clumped hoe, perhaps? But no. Even if that was possible, it would take hours of noisy work, and it would only signal to the servants that she has chosen the wrong side.

By the sound of Patrick's caterwauling, the little snake has bitten him, meaning he likely has hours, not days. Dez knows that rattlesnakes are the most dangerous snakes in Georgia, and also that younger specimens don't control their venom as carefully. Whatever is happening inside that box is beyond her capacity to help. She shuts the heavy wooden door of the suite behind her, and the screams are almost entirely muffled. That's one thing about quality — it has a way of making unpleasant things conveniently disappear.

Out in the hall, she follows the line of servants. They drift together and separately with a sort of comfortable intimacy, bumping into one another or clumping up. No one speaks; everyone carries a weapon.

Ah, yes. Because they're a family, aren't they? Growing up amid a mass of second-best Ruskins, everyone must be either a sibling or a cousin, an aunt or an uncle. These people, this island — it's all they have. All they know.

Well, not really. They know about the outside world. They want it for themselves.

As she follows them, they pass a clock that suggests it's after midnight. Dez perks up, wondering if the Coast Guard might be on their way...

But when they enter Marie's enormous suite, the windows have been scrubbed clean. So much for any chance of rescue. Marie sees it, too. In the media, she's known for her iron backbone, her disinterest in compromise, her high standards, her absolute confidence in the fashion world. But now her shoulders slump, her head falls forward. She could be any woman in her late fifties — well, any woman in her late fifties who's had thousands of dollars of plastic surgery, who has hair and makeup artists on staff, who has a personal chef at each of her homes, and who owns a priceless wardrobe bolstered by only the finest shapewear.

"In here?" Marie asks, nose scrunched in disgust. "On my own bed? Are you going to treat me like Christiane?"

"Of course not. You're not carrying another Ruskin. I've actually given you a lot of thought." Valerie throws herself on

Marie's enormous bed. The mattress must be hard — she doesn't bounce. "We almost built a guillotine just for you. Because here's the thing, Mom…"

A pause to let that barb strike home —

But Marie doesn't flinch.

"The men I can understand. They know what's happening when they're chosen as boys. They jockey for it. And when they get it, they're ready to reap all their rewards, to take every advantage being a Ruskin offers them. Sex and money. That's all they want, really. And power, but they've never lived without it, so they take it for granted."

She stands up and walks to Marie. Dez can see the resemblance — the Ruskin eyes, hair, and coloring, combined with Marie's button nose and high cheekbones. They are exactly the same height.

"But you had options. You *chose* this. You signed the NDA." Valerie looks to Dez. "Not just the one to get on the Island, but the big one. You've never seen a marriage contract like this, I promise." She refocuses on Marie. "You come from a good family. You were already born wealthy. But you knowingly signed away your daughters. You entered this family knowing that you would be required to produce heirs and knowing that the ones that came out of you might not be the ones you claimed. The ones you raised." She steps closer, right in Marie's face now. "The one thing a mother is supposed to do is love her babies, and you gave up two daughters, traded them for sons so you could go on running a stupid little magazine."

Internally, Dez flinches. When she agreed to come here, working at *Nouveau* was the greatest goal of her life. She was willing to do anything — *anything!* — to get that byline on her resume. But now, those glossy pages might as well be tinder for a fire. She wanted Marie as a boss, wanted to learn from her, but now she doesn't want to breathe the same air as her. This woman threw her daughters away, damned them to a life of rape and servitude, all for some words and pretty pictures on a page. If there is one thing that Dez has never, ever doubted, it's her mother's love — something Valerie never got.

Valerie turns on her heel and sashays to a mirrored coffee table. A spray of *Nouveau* issues sits beside a cracked-glass vase of delicate roses, a perfect ballerina pink. She picks up one of the magazines and flips through it. "Oh! This year's color is banana, and wide-leg jeans are in fashion again. Thank God we can let everyone know." She throws the magazine against the wall. "You're telling me my life is an equal trade for that shit? How fucking dare you."

"Someone has been feeding you lies," Marie says tiredly. "You're not my daughter. I never had any daughters."

Valerie's head snakes around, her eyes narrowing. "Why should I believe you? Do you seriously think I'm that stupid? I share your fucking genes. All the brains, none of the opportunities." She looks down, breathes out through her nose, composing herself. "We found the records. They look remarkably like the ones in the stables. Champion fucking bloodlines."

Marie goes white upon hearing this, her eyes darting around the room, hunting for escape or a weapon, Dez would assume.

"Desirée," Marie says, looking right at her as if seeing her for the first time, her voice pleading. "You can't trust them. These people — they don't know the truth. They just want to take what's not theirs. I've seen your work. I know you're a gifted designer, that you have aspirations in fashion. I can help with that. I can take you under my wing with the magazine, get you in with the best fashion houses. You can have full run of my wardrobe — "

Valerie walks to a pair of white double doors and throws them open to show an all-white walk-in closet the size of a suite. The built-ins are immaculate, the shoes are showcased in dramatically lit boxes, and the dresses wait in rainbow order on white wooden hangers. A chandelier hangs down, glittering like the sun, and the white carpet looks like spun sugar. Dez can imagine running her hands over the dresses, touching actual couture, considering each hand-sewn label. There are enough Birkins in that closet to fund her entire future, enough Birkins to buy the shitty apartment complex her mom barely manages to live in. If she had the combination to the safe buried in the wall, she could probably buy the Island by selling the jewelry inside.

She feels like a child in a candy store.

And yet...

There is no escape here, is there?

Every person here who is not a servant has died tonight, everyone except her and Marie, and judging by Valerie's rage with the woman she believes to be her mother, Dez knows Marie doesn't have long.

No matter what Marie says, she cannot secure a future for Dez at her magazine.

She can't even secure her own future five minutes from now.

It's a pathetic little ploy on Marie's part.

"The thing she hasn't realized yet," Valerie says to Dez as if they're gal pals, "is that you don't need her to enjoy the contents of her closet. It's right there, and her hands are tied. Go on in. Take whatever you want."

Dez looks at the closet. At Marie. At the servants silently ringing the room.

At Valerie.

"What's the point?" Dez says. "You're just going to kill me. So, what — I go into the closet and fill up my arms like it's *Supermarket Sweep*, and then you guys shoot me for being greedy? I wanted a job, not a Birkin. And I can't work a job if I'm dead on this stupid fucking Fantasy Island where I definitely don't belong."

Valerie actually smiles. "See, I knew I liked you. I told the girls in the kitchen the other night that it was such a shame Patrick brought you along this time in particular. Just spectacularly bad luck, you know?"

"So I'm learning."

Dez's stomach grumbles in protest, and a few titters go up around the room.

"We can't let you live," Valerie admits. "You've just seen too much. And even if you believe you'll never tell, we've watched enough cop shows to know how interrogation tactics work. None of us are willing to take the fall because you got waterboarded."

Dez heaves a sigh. "Yeah. I get it."

"Are you actually on their side?" Marie bellows. "After all they've done, can you really not see that they're monsters? They're going to kill you, Desirée. You have to fight back."

"They're not monsters," Dez tells her. "You're the only monster that's left. I'm just collateral damage."

After a long moment of chilly silence, Marie holds up her pearl-wrapped wrists and says, "Then get it over with. Kill us off and steal lives you don't deserve. Ungrateful bastards."

Valerie's smile now is disturbing. She looks like she's just had an idea that absolutely delights her. Dez has seen enough tonight to know that's a very bad thing.

"We were going to cover you in *Nouveau* and furs and use you to start the fire," Valerie says to Marie. "But now I've got a better idea. You both go in the closet." She gestures to the gleaming space of dreams.

"If you kill Marie, maybe we'll let you live."

22

"Does anyone object?" Valerie asks.

No one says a word.

She claps her hands and points. "Then go ahead."

Dez looks around the room, shrugs, and walks into the closet, standing there dumbly. She is well aware of the discrepancy between her secondhand athleisure, her destroyed makeup, her ragged hair, and the glorious perfection within. She's been aware of it all her life. She is still the little girl who scavenged old lipsticks left behind in hotel rooms and used a toothpick to scrape out the last swipe of sumptuously bright red.

Valerie pushes Marie into the closet and stares at them for a moment.

"Good luck." She winks at Dez and closes the double doors.

For a long moment, they stand there, not quite side by side. Marie steps close to the door, listening intently.

"I don't think they can hear us," she whispers. "Now untie me, and let's get out of here."

Dez looks around. "What, is there a secret panel in here or something?"

A snort of derision. "Of course there is. You've heard of a panic room? We obviously have one."

But Dez does not tell Marie that she has already visited one panic room, and that it's already out of service. She does not help Marie extricate herself from the pearls wrapped around her wrists. "Where is it?"

"Untie me, and I'll show you."

"Show me, and I'll untie you."

The glare Marie gives her tells Dez exactly the kind of boss she might've been, in a different universe where they simply had a nice if dispassionate family dinner instead of watching a series of carefully planned revenge murders.

"Fine," Marie finally says, because they both know who has the power here, even if it is the tiniest, barest sliver of power.

Marie walks to the far wall, her bare feet sinking into the carpet. She shields whatever she's doing with her body so that Dez can't see it — like it even matters — and Dez prepares herself for a hidden panel to swing out and reveal a very posh steel box fitted with a wine fridge and a year's supply of caviar.

But nothing happens.

"Goddammit," Marie growls. "This is supposed to be easy!"

Dez smothers her laugh.

Yes, living on your own private island is supposed to be *easy*.

But here they are.

Marie spins around.

"You try it. There's a latch right here. My stupid hands…"

When Marie moves aside, Dez takes her place. The latch is well hidden, but when she finds it, it doesn't budge.

Her hopes fall, not that they were very high. So far, the servants have been one step ahead, every time.

"I guess they disabled it? Disarmed it? Whatever the word is. They've been planning this for a long time. They weren't just going to leave a panic room intact. And if they did, they'd just fill it with scorpions or something," Dez says.

When she turns around, Marie is giving her a measuring look, almost a look of approval. "You know, you're a sharp young woman. Under different circumstances, I would've enjoyed championing your career."

Last week, Dez would've given a pinky toe to hear this from her idol. But now, after all that she's seen — including destroyed pinky toes — the words sound hollow.

"Really? Because you didn't speak to me until there were dead bodies all around us. In fact, it seemed like you were avoiding me, back when things were going according to plan."

Something swims in Marie's eyes, wary and calculating. "I'm leery of anyone my boys bring home. We get so many gold diggers, so many sycophants who want to worm their way into the family. I generally remain distant at first, until I see who they really are."

"You could at least introduce yourself. Even before all the killing, this place was creepy as fuck."

Marie's jaw drops in affront. "Creepy? The Island is considered one of the most sumptuous homes in the entire world."

A snort. "I'll take friendly, normal people who actually speak at dinner and give awkward hugs over... whatever that was." She stands up taller. "And you know what? Patrick is a douchebag. Just an absolute prick. Selfish, snobby, stupid. I can't believe you'd choose him over someone like Valerie."

Marie rolls her eyes. "Oh, you think I got to choose? That's terribly amusing. Haven't you been listening? I may call the shots in my New York office, but out here, I don't even get to choose what to wear to dinner; Grandmother does that. Out here, I'm just as much a pawn and puppet as anyone else. That's the price you pay for power in the real world. You can't get ahead without sacrifice. If you don't believe that, just ask a politician." She looks around the room, considering. "Now, if you untie me, maybe we can use something in here as a weapon. Or I could bribe them with the code to the safe, maybe?"

"I don't think they're doing this for the money."

"Oh, you little fool. Once we're gone, do you think they'll let it go? They want a taste of the good life, the one they think they've been denied. Just wait until they see the legal documents around the trust. They'll get nothing. Because they are nothing." She holds out her wrists. "Now, for the love of God, untie me."

Dez doesn't budge.

"Why? Why should I do that? They said that if I kill you, I can maybe get out of here. Why would I make it easier for you to fight back?"

Marie's face rearranges itself into an entirely different person, the one in the society papers and in the front row at Fashion

Week. Her eyes are lit warmly, her smile fond and welcoming. Dez feels like a sunbeam is ensconcing her in a golden glow, like she's suddenly being seen as she's always hoped to be seen.

"Darling, I don't want to fight you. I want to fight them off together. You have spunk. And talent. I need people like you. We can do this, but only if we do it *together*."

Dez... bursts out laughing.

"Wow, Marie. Wow. That was like watching an alien pretend to be human. You almost had me, actually. Man, does this family turn people into sociopaths, or do they only let sociopaths into the club? Because *damn*, that was impressive."

Marie's face shifts again, a chameleon changing color, and she's a calculating reptile again. "Both, I suspect." She cocks her head. "I suppose we're at an impasse. Here's the thing, though. I know things you don't know, and you can't kill me. Because you need me."

Dez chuckles at how ridiculous this sounds coming from a woman who can't use her hands. "Doubtful. Very doubtful."

"I know who your father is, Desirée Margaret Lane. Your mother's been lying to you. And if you want a secure future after these stupid little games are over, you're going to want to know the full truth."

23

That... gets Dez's attention.

Her mother is a good mother, but she has always claimed not to know who Dez's father is, and when asked, has grown angry and evasive and assured Dez that what's in the past is in the past, and that every young woman makes mistakes and should be allowed to forget them.

Dez swore to herself that she would never make such mistakes, that she would never saddle herself with a child she could barely support.

Now she realizes that her mistake was using Patrick.

She played a stupid game, and she has won a stupid prize.

If she'd just been patient or done a little brainstorming, she wouldn't be here, in this hellmansion, fighting for her life. She'd be at home sewing bugle buttons onto an old dress, full of hope, waiting for an email. Hell, maybe the email came while she was here.

Maybe she's been offered an interview and she doesn't even know it because they took away her phone.

"How could you possibly know who my father is, and what good will that knowledge do me if I untie you and you kill me?" she asks.

Marie manages to look smug and carefree despite her current, inelegant state. She smiles the smile of an alley cat that's down on hard times but is quite certain she'll be eating tuna in someone's kitchen very soon.

"Do you think we let just anyone on this island? Oh, no. We don't take chances on people who don't have the correct genes." She reaches over, and Dez jerks away from her. Marie holds up a long, peachy hair plucked from Dez's black shirt. "DNA is so easy to find, you know."

"You had Patrick steal my hair so you could run a DNA test on me?" Dez's mouth is all watery, like she would throw up if she could. This is such a horrific intrusion. They have stolen some small piece of her body, and now someone else owns the knowledge of every secret part of her, inside and out.

"Of course. You would've noticed if he'd asked you to spit into a tube, but you left several hairs in his car, which we took to our lab. And I must say we were all surprised at the results. We assumed you were just another ragged little mutt willing to debase yourself for the chance at a life of luxury, and instead, you were the most compelling horse in the race." She raises an eyebrow and holds up her wrists, shaking the pearls. "Don't you want to know, Desirée? Aren't you at least a little bit curious? He's important, your father. *Very* important. And rich."

Dez considers her, ponders how to play this bizarre game to get what she wants. And then she realizes… there is no longer a reason for any masks. They can be perfectly honest. No matter what Marie may believe, no matter what Marie may want Dez to think, only one of them can leave this closet alive.

"I'm not a gold digger," she says, reaching out to tug at the tightly tied pearls, each perfect little silk knot making the string impossibly strong. "All I wanted was a job. I don't want success handed to me. I just want a foot in the door. A chance to prove myself. I know I'm talented. But — and you may actually be familiar with this problem — there are quite a few barriers to entry for those not born into a wealthy family."

"About that — " Marie tries to interrupt, smooth as a snake.

"Yeah, I know, my dad. Whatever. Point being, I never wanted Patrick. I didn't want to marry him and become part of — of whatever this is. There is nothing in the world worth putting up with the monster you raised. I would not hitch my wagon to that flaming sack of shit you call a son. I only came here because I wanted to meet you. Because I admire what you've accomplished. I read every fawning article about you pulling yourself up by your bootstraps. And I used to think you did it all by yourself."

The pearls shift, the knot beginning to loosen as she gently works it free. Marie shifts, too, her stance a little less demure, a little more balanced, a predator readying herself for the next pounce.

"And now I know you didn't do shit. You sold off your daughters, raised someone else's sons, and allowed them to become assholes, all while looming over the fashion world like some kind of god. But you weren't a god. You were just another person who had the money to get whatever they wanted. And you know what?"

Dez looks up, locks eyes with Marie.

"Banana isn't the next 'it' color. It's ugly as fuck."

The pearls are almost loose now, and Marie is wiggling her fingers, getting her blood pumping again. Dez is fairly certain she knows what Marie will do the moment she's free: she can see Marie's eyes darting to a very particular part of the closet. Much like her son when he sees something he wants, the woman is not subtle.

"Banana will be the next 'it' color because I say it is." Marie jerks her hands apart, and the pearls finally fall to the ground.

24

There is one long, silent second of tension, and then Marie lunges for the sharpest heels on the shelves — a pair of sky-high stilettos that could cut steak. Dez kneels, grabbing the dropped pearl necklace and pulling the long, circular string taut between her hands. While Marie is focused on the shoes, Dez flips the pearls over that once-perfect platinum bob and jerks the gleaming strand back against Marie Caulfield-Ruskin's unnaturally smooth neck.

Marie has a black Louboutin heel in hand, but Dez yanks her backward like she's pulling the reins on a horse. Marie flails, trying and failing to hit Dez with the shoe, and Dez gathers all the strength left in her body and pulls the older woman to the ground.

Landing hard on her back, Marie sucks in a deep breath as the pearls fall loose against her chest. She has perhaps two inches and ten pounds on Dez but is still a petite woman, and despite that article about her 'addiction' to the gym in *Cosmo*,

Dez is fairly certain she doesn't generally lift anything heavier than a glass of red wine. Marie scrambles to her hands and knees, whooping in big breaths of air, and Dez again gets the pearls around her neck — but this time, Dez straddles her back like a jockey, clinging on for dear life.

"Your father — " Marie gasps.

Dez winds the pearls together and starts twisting them, cutting off whatever Marie had to say on that topic as she cuts off her air.

"Let me guess," Dez whispers in her ear. "If you say I'm actually a blueblood instead of what you consider a mutt, if you now think I'm a viable candidate for your creepy-ass eugenics breeding program on this island, that means my dad is someone important from old money. Let me guess. It's Ronald Tower. He owns the hotel where my mom has worked since I was born, and he's got the bloodlines and the money. Am I right? Is that the carrot you've been dangling to keep me from killing you?"

"Father — " Marie croaks.

She drops the show and digs her fingers into the pearls cutting into her throat, but they're too tight to give her any purchase. Dez keeps twisting them tighter and tighter. Her hands hurt, her fingers are red from the tension.

"What did you say, Marie? Whatever. I'm going to assume that's a yes."

Marie can't speak, can't even get enough air to groan. She scrabbles at her neck with both perfectly manicured hands, then drops back down to all fours, then falls forward onto her belly.

Dez doesn't let go, doesn't let up. She doesn't care if it cuts off circulation to every finger she has and they shrivel up and drop off like blackened plums, she's not going to let this spoiled bitch go.

Now on the ground, Marie's head turns to the side, one blue eye staring up at Dez, the white going red with burst blood vessels and her tan, perfectly powdered cheek turning the exact shade of mauve that was *Nouveau*'s 2021 Color of the Year. Marie's fingers dig into the fluffy carpet, her body bucking under Dez like an antelope under a lion.

Twist.

Twist.

Twist.

In this moment, Dez is infinitely aware of every detail in their surroundings, as if time has stretched out forever and each second feels like an hour. She smells the fake linen scent pumped in from a plug-in, realizes that a bit of shadow on the wall means one of the bulbs in the chandelier is out. She notices the patterns in the beading on Marie's dress and thinks about the women who were paid a pittance to sew each bead on by hand, screamed at by a manager who makes ten times more than they do so that the dress can be sold by a designer who makes ten times more than that manager so that it can be bought by someone for whom money is no object.

Is this really the life she wanted so badly?

Did she really want to dedicate her time on the planet to making clothes for assholes like Marie Caulfield-Ruskin?

Did she really think couture was anything more than a sequined celebrity circle jerk for the sake of money laundering?

If she lives through this, Dez might have an existential crisis.

Twist.

Twist.

Twist.

Marie goes still beneath her.

Dez does not let go.

She has seen too many horror movies to assume that, just because a body isn't breathing, it isn't still capable of turning on her.

She counts three hundred seconds of absolute stillness, three hundred thumps of her blood in the veins of her aching fingers.

And then she lets go.

25

Before she attempts to stand, Dez kicks the stiletto that Marie dropped in their struggle well out of reach.

And then she carefully, painfully releases the pearls. They've made perfect indents in the soft flesh of her fingers, leaving them misshapen and red. She shakes them out, puts two fingers to Marie's neck, and finds no pulse. She holds her palm under Marie's mouth and feels no breath. Her legs wobble under her as she finds her way upright. She looks down at what she has done and only wishes that there was some way to be sure that Marie is gone, that she can't suddenly pop upright like the killers always do in slasher films.

But there are no weapons here, there are no —

Oh.

Dez picks up the shoe Marie considered a possible murder weapon. It's a black snakeskin Louboutin stiletto with a sky-high heel, that telltale crimson sole utterly unmarred by use. It doesn't even look like it's ever been worn. A thirty-eight; just one size bigger than her own. She holds it up to her nose, inhales the rich scent. She always imagined a new Louboutin would smell this way.

She kicks over Marie with her worn sneakers, sneakers that have touched every vile thing on the hot Savannah sidewalk. What she's going to do now — she doesn't want to do it. But she knows it must be done. It must be final. It must be forever.

With Marie Caulfield-Ruskin on her back, Dez tugs off her sneaker and her filthy, stinky, sweaty, blood-crusted sock, and she slips her bare foot into the Louboutin like Cinderella finally finding her glass slipper. She puts the heel over Marie's throat, and Marie's eyes fly open.

26

The decision is a sudden one, barely any thought at all, like dancing around with a mouse cavorting underfoot, like batting away a bug. The Louboutin's high, sharp heel is in place, and Dez puts her full weight on it, stepping down with all her might.

The feeling of flesh under her foot is one Dez could never possibly forget — the way it's soft and then oddly hard as it punches through, the way the shoe lands on solid ground on the other side. The heel doesn't hit the trachea or the spine, just goes through the — the soft bits. The sound is a tearing sort of pop, almost quiet, like such an expensive shoe doesn't wish to offend. The blood burbles up, but not quite a gush, not a fountain. It's soaking into the fluffy white carpet. There's almost a… politeness about it.

The blue eyes quiver, and the light leaves them.

Dez sees it, the moment it happens.

Marie is not getting up again.

Stepping out of the coveted shoe, leaving it pinning Marie to the floor like a prized butterfly, Dez hobbles to the closed closet door.

"It's done," she says softly. And then louder, "It's done!"

The door opens, and Valerie is standing there, smiling. "How'd you do it?" she asks. "We didn't hear a scuffle. Please tell me she got what she deserved."

Dez steps aside to reveal her work, almost with pride. She's not quite here in her body right now, she's floating somewhere else, bobbing about like a balloon along the intensely detailed, aggressively white crown molding, and that's okay. She doesn't need to be here. She did what she had to do. She's been doing it since she saw Uncle Frank claimed by the sharks. Hell, maybe even before then. Maybe all her life.

People without this kind of money, without *enough* money — they just keep on going, no matter what.

"Perfection," Valerie says.

And then, much to Dez's surprise, Valerie draws her into a hug.

"Are you going to kill me?" Dez asks in a tiny voice, just now realizing that she's shaking.

"We don't have to." Valerie steps back, holds her at arm's length. "Now you're just as guilty as we are. Give us away, you give yourself away. We're even."

Hearing that, Dez bursts out crying.

Valerie pulls her close, like she actually means it.

Time speeds up after that. Two of the men pick up Marie's body and carry it out of the closet. Dez wonders what they're doing, wonders if they will leave the shoe obscenely inside her, but Valerie leads her downstairs to the kitchen where they first met and, of all things, hands her a banana, which Dez gulps down too fast. Someone else hands her a water bottle, and she mumbles her thanks and drinks the whole thing so she won't choke on the clumps of banana stuck in her throat. She does not want to vomit up the next color of the year.

"What now?" she asks, once she can breathe again.

The two women sit at the table together like old friends, and for all the horrible things Dez has seen Valerie do today, she suddenly, finally feels like she's exactly where she belongs.

"We were raised to work," Valerie says, biting into an apple. "So we have to work for one more night. We'll move all the bodies out to the yacht and clean up every sign of the violence that happened here. Abigail is scrubbing the blood off the counter, and Leo and Ed are sledgehammering the concrete, and someone else is bleaching Marie's carpet, and the grooms are tending to the ponies. When we're done, there will be no sign of anything untoward on the Island. Believe me — we know how to make that happen. Tomorrow morning, the yacht will explode and catch fire because Uncle Frank got stupid with a cigar again, and everything will sink to the bottom of the sea with all the old Ruskins on board."

"But what about you?" Dez asks. "What about the children. Are they — did you — ?"

"Oh, no. Never. We're not like them." Valerie's smile is gentler than Dez ever imagined. "The nice thing about keeping meticulous secret records of your — " she makes finger quotes " — *secret breeding program* is that once the secret part disappears, the records are still good. We can prove that we are who we say we are. DNA tests don't lie. And as for the children..." She looks out the window, toward the shifting blue waves. "They're in the servants' quarters — where we live. It's hidden on the back side of the house because people like you are never supposed to see it. That's where the kids have always stayed until their fates are decided, where the ones who lose the lottery learn a new set of rules. There are plenty of people ready to love them, ready to raise them to be exactly who they are instead of who they're expected to become." She looks into Dez's eyes. "It's going to be touch and go for Christiane's baby. A girl, so tiny..."

"It's better this way," Dez finishes for her. "Maybe she'll actually have a chance."

Valerie nods. "I'm glad we didn't kill you."

Dez nods, tears in her eyes. "Me too."

With a determined sigh, Valerie stands. "I've got to go help out. You can go sleep in your room, if you want. Things are going to get really busy in the morning, so it would be best if you told whoever shows up that you weren't feeling well and skipped the breakfast on the yacht to sleep. Just feign ignorance." Her hand strays to the heavy lump in her apron pocket. "We really can trust you, right? To not tell? Because as long as the Ruskin estate stands, your NDA actually covers all this. No one can force you to say anything. Even the police. Even the FBI."

Dez chuckles sadly, thinking about what an innocent idiot she was when she signed those papers.

"I'm not telling anybody. They got what they deserved." She exhales and wonders if her hands will ever stop shaking. "But what about you? What will you do now?"

"We're not sure how it will play out exactly, but we have access to plenty of undocumented cash and sellables. The ultimate goal is to get to the mainland and live regular lives, but…" She gazes out the window, her brow furrowed. "There are lots of challenges there. Legally, we don't exist. No birth certificates, no ID, no real schooling after age five. But whatever happens, it has to be better than this."

"I don't know how much help I would be, but I'm here if you need me," Dez says. "I can give you my number."

"That's really sweet. We already have your number, though. We know everything about you, actually. Bill's people are very good at digging up that kind of thing." Valerie nods and heads for the door, where she stops, one hand on the jamb. "Speaking of which… do you want to know who your dad is? We have the paperwork."

"Oh. Huh." Dez sits back in her chair, considering it. She's fairly certain she already knows the answer; she told Marie the truth. "No. Maybe just destroy that, too. I think I'm done with the uber wealthy. It just seems like they're all assholes."

"Most aren't as bad as this, but some are," Valerie admits. "And most of them have visited this island to play polo. I'll have your papers shredded." With a little wave, she disappears. Dez has spent all night running away from Valerie, but now…

Now she wishes they could actually be friends.

She finishes the bottle of water and trudges up to her room. It's still pitch dark outside, early morning, and the servants are everywhere, picking up shards of broken glass and mopping up bloodstains with paper towels. Everything smells like lemon. A gurgle in the ceiling suggests the water has been turned on again. Dez wonders why everyone is still wearing their uniforms, but... well, they can change after they're done with one last clean, can't they? They must have other clothes, somewhere. Or maybe they'll raid the many wardrobes and walk-in closets, once all the blood is scrubbed away. If she were one of them, she would never wear pink again.

In her room, she peels off her sweaty leggings and shirt and steps into the shower. The hot water sends her mind elsewhere, and then she wakes up sitting on the white marble tile, the water pounding against her back, her chin on her knees. She is just now starting to realize that she killed someone with her own bare hands.

That she is a murderer.

And she can't ever tell anyone, not even a therapist.

This is something she'll have to work through on her own.

It's something she does not regret.

So there's that, and then there's the existential crisis of realizing that her life's dream is now... well, not out of reach, but something she no longer wants. The only people who can afford couture are exactly the kind of people she wishes to avoid. Maybe she'll look into athleisure or costuming or... literally anything with fashion that won't involve working for someone like Marie Caulfield-Ruskin.

Dez dries off with an enormous towel, puts on fresh pajamas, and goes through the comforting rigor of her complex curly hair routine. She wonders if Patrick is still alive in that box just a few doors down the hall, and how the servants will collect his body without suffering their own bites from the snake, and where the roaches will go. They could've just shot everyone in the head and called it a night, but instead, the servants made their tormentors suffer, thereby making their own cleanup even more difficult.

That's what years of abuse and resentment will do, apparently.

When she emerges from the bathroom, she finds the black snakeskin Louboutin stilettos sitting neatly on her bed. They've been meticulously cleaned; the only red is the telltale crimson sole.

Next to the shoes is a pink sticky note with familiar handwriting in plain black ink.

Spoils of war, it says.

She picks up the right shoe, remembering how it felt on her foot, stomping down with all her might. Dez once thought she would do anything to reach her ambitions.

Now she knows exactly how far she'll go.

ACKNOWLEDGEMENTS

Thanks to Cath Trechman for trusting me on what might be my zaniest pitch of all time.

Thanks to everyone at Titan for creating such a beautiful book. Thanks to Julia Lloyd for another banger of a cover, to Adrian McLaughlin for book design, and to the publicity and marketing team who work so hard to get the word out, including Katharine Carroll, Kabriya Coghlan, Kate Greally, Charlotte Kelly, and Isabelle Sinnott.

Thanks to my fierce agent, Stacia Decker. I'm pretty sure you would escape the island.

Thanks to everyone who read an advance copy and offered kind words, including V. Castro, Gabino Iglesias, T. Kingfisher, Eric LaRocca, Clay McLeod Chapman, Katrina Monroe, Rory Power, Chuck Wendig, and Ally Wilkes.

Thanks, as always, to my husband Craig who showed me the dark underbelly of Savannah and the glimmering islands that lie across the swamps.

Thanks to Claudette Dorsey for answering my questions about corpses.

Thanks to everyone who picked up a copy of *Bloom* and especially those who reviewed it or told a friend.

And thanks to you, dear reader, for giving this book a chance. I hope you love it and buy a copy for someone who needs some bloody catharsis. Or for a boss who needs a *hint*.

ABOUT THE AUTHOR

Delilah S. Dawson is the *New York Times*-bestselling and Stoker Award®-nominated author of *Bloom*, *The Violence*, *Mine*, *Camp Scare*, the Blud series, the Hit series, *Servants of the Storm*, *Midnight at the Houdini*, several Star Wars books, and the Shadow series, written as Lila Bowen. As a child, she cleaned offices alongside her parents' janitorial service and once ate day-old birthday cake out of a bank's kitchen trash, so that's who you're dealing with.

Find her online at www.delilahsdawson.com and on social media, @delilahsdawson.

For more fantastic fiction, author events,
exclusive excerpts, competitions, limited editions and more

VISIT OUR WEBSITE
titanbooks.com

LIKE US ON FACEBOOK
facebook.com/titanbooks

FOLLOW US ON TWITTER AND INSTAGRAM
@TitanBooks

EMAIL US
readerfeedback@titanemail.com